BOSTON
PUBLIC
LIBRARY

D1161190

STILL WATERS

A NOVEL OF SUSPENSE

KERRY TUCKER

HarperCollins*Publishers*

FIRST EDITION

Designed by Helene Berinsky

Library of Congress Cataloging-in-Publication Data

Tucker, Kerry.
    Still waters : a novel of suspense / Kerry Tucker. — 1st ed.
        p. cm.
    ISBN 0-06-016529-4
    I. Title.
    PS3570.U34S75   1991
    813'.54—dc20   90-55572

91 92 93 94 95 MV/HC 10 9 8 7 6 5 4 3 2 1

For Hal

ACKNOWLEDGMENTS

For advice on technical matters, thank you to Richard Tucker, Ph.D., of the Bowman Gray School of Medicine in Winston-Salem, North Carolina; Weezie Morgan, V.M.D., of the Brewster Animal Clinic in Brewster, Massachusetts; Ann G. Harris, C.P.G., of the Department of Geology, Youngstown State University, Youngstown, Ohio; Howard K. Stearns, Inspector with the Watertown Fire Department in Watertown, Massachusetts; and Margueritte Shingler of the East Liverpool Museum of Ceramics in East Liverpool, Ohio, which, unlike the fictional Marshall County Historical Society Museum, is orderly, lively, and well-lighted.

Thank you also to Kate Mattes, Jed Mattes, Larry Ashmead, Eamon Dolan, Brenda Marsh, and Lori Marsh.

Beneath still waters
    there's a strong undertow,
The surface won't tell you
    what the deep water knows.

Dallas Frazier, "Beneath Still Waters"

Anybody can kill anybody.

Lynette "Squeaky" Fromme

STILL WATERS

1

The phone rang for the third time in ten minutes. I wedged the receiver between my shoulder and ear and continued to shake my tank of developing fluid with both hands, rather violently.

"Hugh," I said, "I can't talk about it anymore. I'm not writing any phony letter to any landlord saying we're married so you can have cheap rent for the rest of your life, so just lay off."

Hugh was driving me nuts. We hadn't talked in the six months since I'd walked out on him, and for a good six months before that. Now that the guy who owned the apartment Hugh and I used to share was talking about kicking him out at the end of the lease, he couldn't stop calling me. Messages on the machine, messages at work, calls in the morning and, now, at night, when he knew I was in the darkroom. The right to live in a three-room rent-controlled apartment on Manhattan's Upper West Side is probably the only thing in the world he would lay down his life for.

"I'm not Hugh," said the voice, deep and unfamiliar. "Is this Olivia Kincaid?"

"Yes, it is," I said. "That is, I'm Libby Kincaid."

The "Olivia" made me nervous. Nobody called me that except my father, when he was a little drunk and dreamy, and my brother, when he wanted to make me mad. I switched off the radio. The sound of sirens and barking dogs rose up from Canal Street, swarmed through the loft, and penetrated the darkroom door.

"Are you Avery Kincaid's sister?" he said. "We took two days trying to find you. I don't know how to say what I have to say."

It was eighty degrees and as still as an oven in the room, but I felt a breeze skim across my shoulders.

"Yes, I am," I said, surprised at the catch in my voice. "What's wrong?"

I didn't need to listen to what he said; I knew before he opened his mouth. Avery was dead.

Words came out of the receiver. The funeral would be tomorrow afternoon; I'd fly to Ohio in the morning.

Another spoke was gone from the wheel.

2

The funeral service took place in a small Lutheran church with robin's-egg-blue walls and varnished black pews. The minister, who was the father of one of Avery's high school students, said three times in his sermon that Avery had "returned himself to God," reminded us that Avery had enjoyed fishing, bowling, and the company of students, and gave us mimeographed directions to the cemetery. It was on a hillside about a mile away from the house where Avery and I lived as children. We used hold our breath when we rode by; according to a childhood maxim, whoever breathed when passing a cemetery would be the next to die. Now most of my family is buried there.

The hill was bronze with dead grass and dormant shrubbery; the gravestones, drenched from three days of rain, were dark as steel.

As the pallbearers lowered Avery's coffin into the ground, I resisted a tremendous urge to take a picture. All day my fingers had curled and uncurled around the camera slung at my side. What kept me from raising it to my eye now was an unfamiliar sense of decorum, and probably fear that everyone would look at me even harder than they already had.

They started shoveling the dirt on and I turned away, hoping to get back to the road and to Avery's pickup truck before anyone tried to talk to me. I concentrated on the ground so I wouldn't have to see any more faces. The dirt was soft and wet and sucked at my feet as I walked down the shallow hillside; my last Kleenex was a hard wad in my jacket pocket.

I was a hundred feet away from the pickup when I noticed that someone was sitting in the passenger seat. He must have been watching me approach in the mirror, because as soon as I saw him he opened the door and got out. He was wearing a red plaid jacket and brown pants, and there was something unnervingly familiar about the way he held one arm across his chest and with his other hand held a cigarette to his mouth.

The man was my father. I'd last seen him three years before, when I'd spent a month in Ohio shooting abandoned steel mills for *Americans*, the magazine I work for. He was living in Kentucky then—or at least that's what his license plates had said. Somehow he'd gotten word of Avery's death.

Who told him these things? What kind of moldy old grapevine made it its business to pass news on to him?

I hugged him, like I always do.

"Hey, Dad, let's just go for a ride."

I watched the crowd at Avery's grave break up into groups of two and three and begin to move down the hillside toward the cars. He saw them too.

"Okay," he said, "but I'm kind of pushed for time."

I swung out into the road, the gravel crackling beneath the truck's tires. Dad pulled another cigarette from a dented package and lit up.

I turned too sharply onto the highway at the end of the cemetery road; a thicket of witch hazel scrubbed the side of the pickup.

"Jesus, girl," he said.

We drove past cowfields, then the Webster dairy, then a jalopy of a house covered in asphalt shingles, its windows boarded shut.

Let him talk first, I said to myself. You always do the talking. Make him talk first.

But of course he didn't.

I rolled down the window and tried to breathe deeply. The air smelled like fall. A mixture of fermenting leaves, wet dirt, and cows.

"How did you get to the cemetery?"

"Got a lift."

I couldn't help smiling. He was good at this.

"Are you staying in town?"

"Not for long."

It was like trying to start an old car on a wet day. You keep trying. Give it a little more gas—no, not too much—try it again, then again.

"They say he was depressed because he split up with his girlfriend, and he shot himself in the head."

It caught this time.

"They're full of shit."

This had become his stock description of most of the people in his life: his relatives, my mother's relatives, friends who were mad at him because he owed them money, and his occasional—very occasional—employers.

"Do you know anything I don't know?" I asked.

We rode for a while in silence.

"I feel bad, Dad," I said. "He called me a couple of months ago and said he was feeling pretty low. That he was breaking up with his girlfriend and he needed something to cheer him up. He wanted to come visit me in New York, but I was getting ready to go on the road for a couple of weeks. I couldn't change the assignment; it was too late."

The truth was, I didn't want to give the assignment, which was to take pictures of Jack Nicholson at his place in Aspen, to anyone else.

"I told him I didn't have time—that November or December would be better. He said that was okay, but now I guess it wasn't. He must have been a lot worse off than I thought. I wish I'd known."

He didn't respond, but I didn't expect him to. I'd stopped expecting anything at all from him, including encouragement or consolation, years ago.

"A friend of Avery's from the high school is having people over for dinner. Nothing fancy. Cold cuts or something. Do you want to go?"

"You can take me to Dingo's," he said. "I told you—I'm pushed for time."

I took him to Dingo's, a bar the size of a single-car garage on a squalid little block of one-story enterprises on the west side of town. Dingo's, next to it a stucco bowling alley designed to look like a castle, then a windowless corrugated-steel building with a sign that said ADULT NOVELTIES AND PARTY SUPPLIES, and, around the back, the bus station. What had happened to his car this time? Repossessed? Stolen? Or was it hot in the first place?

"See you around," he said.

As usual, I kissed him on the cheek, which was lean and angular, like Avery's was.

3

Darby, Ohio, is one of a dozen or so hard-luck towns strung along the western edge of a spikelike piece of West Virginia that the surveyors for some reason drove between Ohio and Pennsylvania. When my mother lived there as a child, everybody who wasn't a public servant or a farmer had a job at the Pike-Haskell Pottery Works, and the children went to twelve grades of school in a yellow-brick building that looked like a smaller version of the Pike-Haskell. My grandfather taught history and English there and was the principal for a while. The Pike-Haskell folded when I was four, the same year my mother left my father in Wheeling and moved with eight-year-old Avery and me back to Darby to live with her father. The building was razed, and a combination U-Haul dealership and auto-supply center arose in its place. Avery and I went to elementary school in the former Advent Christian Church, and anybody older than sixth grade was shipped to a consolidated school ten miles away—the school where Avery ended up teaching.

Now there's some strip mining going on, and people either do that or work at the gas company. My grandfather and mother are dead, and so's Avery.

My father is chugging Jack Daniel's with some crony at a bar behind the bus station.

*   *   *

I'd called Claire, my roommate, from New York, right after I received the call about Avery. She was spending the week at her mother's place in Maine. She said she wanted to fly to Darby with me, but I wouldn't let her. Now I wished I had. I was on my way to an address written on a folded-up index card that someone had given me after we left the funeral service at the church, and I wasn't going to know anybody there. And everyone was going to say it was terrible and he seemed so happy and the Lord moves in mysterious ways, and I was going to have to be polite and calm.

It started to rain again—just a little.

I found the third house in on Thurman Road, somebody's idea of new construction—a three-car garage with a slightly larger living section angled out from the back. Someone had planted some skeletal-looking azalea bushes in an effort to conceal the concrete-block foundation. There was a brown Ford Bronco in the driveway with a sunset painted on the back, and a big-wheel tricycle in the middle of the front walk. I parked at the curb and heard another car pull up behind me. Then I walked into the house through the garage.

The party—I guess I shouldn't call it a party: the reception? the event?—was hosted by a teacher from Avery's school named Ted Dallas. He taught geometry and coached football. He had picked me up at the airport and brought me Avery's truck. As Avery's closest friend, he had taken most of the funeral proceedings into his own hands, and I was just as glad. His wife, a blonde a couple of years older than I, maybe around thirty-six, brought me a paper cup full of pink stuff to drink. She had a pretty, all-American-girl sort of face— big, wide-set brown eyes, a nose like Debbie Reynolds', and a delicate chin. She was wearing a blue pants suit, and her hair was pulled into a barrette at her neck.

"Are you Libby?" she said. "I'm Marianne Dallas." And, in a lower voice, "Can you come into the kitchen with me? I need to talk to you."

I followed her into the kitchen. She leaned against the sink and looked like she was screwing up her courage to say something.

"You know about Avery's dog, Lucas, don't you?"

Know about the dog? It was too ghoulish even to think about. When the police showed up at Avery's house, they found Avery, dead at the kitchen table, a handgun by his hand and a bullet in his head. The dog, nearly dead from a gunshot wound, had dragged itself across the linoleum and collapsed by Avery's legs. Ted Dallas had told me the grim details on the drive from the airport to the motel, and I'd read about it again in the *Marshall Post-Gazette* clipping that another one of Avery's teacher friends had given me at the church.

"I know about the dog, Marianne. Is he still alive? Do you know where he is?"

Marianne took a sip of her punch.

"He's still alive. He's at the vet's—Pam Bates'. You know her, don't you? Avery's old girlfriend? She gave him Lucas."

The woman was so agitated by now that she was almost breathless. How could Avery's dog be so hard for her to talk about?

"I never met Pam Bates. But Avery used to talk about her sometimes on the phone."

Marianne poured the rest of her punch down the drain and began to peel the handle from the cup.

"Things are bad enough," she said. "I don't want to make them worse. And Ted says I shouldn't interfere. But I'm worried. I'm very worried." Her voice trailed off.

"Worried about what?"

"Pam and Avery had a big fight—a terrible fight—a couple of months ago. I don't know what it was about, and Avery wouldn't tell me. I just heard the end of it. I was at the front door, bringing a jacket back to Avery that he'd left at our place. I heard somebody throw something and glass breaking. And I heard her say to him, 'I swear to God I'll kill you, I really will.' "

She looked up from her cup. "You think I'm crazy, don't you?"

I thought maybe she was.

"Marianne, are you worried that Pam Bates killed Avery?"

"I don't know. It's just that they had that fight, and, well, people can get out of control when a relationship goes bad."

It didn't really seem crazy to me. It just seemed lame, and a little absurd. Everybody has fights. Everybody breaks up. That's the way it is. And besides, the police said it was suicide.

Ted walked into the room and Marianne suddenly reached into an open cabinet.

"Libby needs an aspirin, honey," she said. "What did we do with the Tylenol?"

Ted shrugged his shoulders. "Heck if I know. We eat about a bottle a day." Then, in a more intimate voice, "Honey, do you know where Kevin is? People are asking about him."

She turned to him. "He took his bike out as soon as we got back from the funeral, and I haven't seen him since."

He frowned, then gave her a quick kiss on the forehead and turned to me. "Lib," he said, "I know we've hardly met, but there are a lot of folks in there in the family room who really want to talk with you. Avery had a lot of real good friends."

He took me by the elbow and propelled me out of the kitchen and down a few stairs into a room with orange shag carpet and a fireplace with a metal eagle over the mantel. There were ten or fifteen people there, roughly half women, half men. Mostly couples, I assumed.

Ted walked me toward a table against one wall. It held big plastic platters of salami and cheese and hard rolls, and a punch bowl full of the pink stuff I had been drinking. The paper tablecloth was dimpled and torn and covered with the pink circles left over when people set down their cups of punch while they put their sandwiches together.

"Marianne's not much of a cook, God love her. Help yourself."

I was surprised by my hunger. I made two sandwiches, put them on a paper plate, filled the crack between them with pretzels, then retreated to a corner by the bookcase. The shelves might as well have been labeled His and Hers. His, the Time-Life series on home repairs and a book called *How to Make a Fortune in Real Estate with No Money Down!* Hers, a plaintive eighteen inches of paperbacks, among them *I'm OK, You're OK; My Mother/My Self; The Women's Room; The Relaxation Response;* and *I'm Dancing as Fast as I Can.*

Ted was dragging some folding chairs over to my corner with one hand. He held two cans of Michelob in the other.

"Marianne hid these under the table. She's on an anti-booze kick."

I finished off my punch and poured the beer into the cup.

"You don't look like Avery," he said.

"I look like my mother," I said. "Avery looks—looked—like Dad."

I'm small-boned, fair, and have reddish-brown hair. My features are, in fact, outrageously dainty—not at all in keeping with the tough-gal photojournalist image that I've spent a dozen years cultivating. My persona is, well, inconsistent at best. I wear a leather jacket and no makeup, but I can't resist earrings. Claire says that I have achieved a delicate balance between Amelia Earhart and Mick Jagger.

Avery, on the other hand, was tall and lean, with blue-black hair, a high-bridged nose, and wide, angular cheekbones. He looked a lot like Dad in the old pictures of Mother and him as newlyweds. Dad used to tell us that he was one—thirty-second Cherokee, and my mother told us he was a liar. At any rate, my father wasn't handsome long. By the time I was seven he drank so much every day that the flesh around his eyes had bloated them practically shut.

Ted was running his index finger around the rim of his beer can. His nails were bitten to the quick, and his fingertips bore faint nicotine stains—one of those things that only a smoker, or an ex-smoker, like me, notices. Ted had the kind of good looks essential to a high school jock—broad shoulders, broad jaw, straight teeth, and short blond hair—but he wasn't aging well. He had begun to go plumpish ten years back, I guessed, and must have started to lose his schoolboy charm at about the same time.

I felt an unexpected pang of sympathy for the man. Here he was, trying to do something helpful for a woman he'd never met, and here I was, remorselessly appraising him, visualizing him locked in the frame of my lens. Would I photograph him with his beer against the wood-look paneling, or would I take Ted and Marianne together, American Gothic–style, with the three-car garage behind them?

"Did you know Avery well?" I asked, surprised at the sincerity in my voice.

"Know Avery? I saw him every day for eight years. We bowled together, went to games together, and heck, the way he watched out for Marianne's kid—you'd think they were brothers, or cousins, or something."

"Thanks," I said. "It makes me feel better to know he had good friends."

He touched my hand, then got up and sat to talk with a couple on the couch.

I was approached by a small, fortyish man, with strands of hair brushed sideways in an effort to conceal his baldness. We shook hands, and he introduced himself as Doug Pope, a lawyer from the bank. He had Avery's will. I was the executrix, but that's okay, he'd do all the work. It would go into "streamlined probate," a nice way of saying it wasn't much of an estate, he said. He gave me his card. Would I stop by sometime soon? And if I stopped by at Avery's, would I, er, be sure not to remove anything?

A couple replaced him. Vince Scannell, the principal at Avery's school, and his wife, Lillian, a home ec teacher. "I only wish he'd come to us first. Maybe we could have helped. Or sent him to professional care. I'm sorry, we didn't know." And would I stop by at the school tomorrow to clean out Avery's desk and collect his things? Scannell drew a map on his napkin. Yes, of course. Tomorrow.

Next came a secretary from the athletic office, with long dark hair, pretty blue eyes, acne scars, and a soft, soft voice. "I'm so sorry. He was an awfully nice guy. I mean, we dated for a while, a little while. He was an awfully nice guy."

The Lutheran minister who'd done the honors at the funeral wrapped his moist, fat hand around mine and leaned closely toward me. "Call me, dear, if you need time to talk."

A pack of teenagers came into the house together, the girls all weepy and hanging on to the boys, the boys in their Sunday suits. They drifted through the room, talked to the teachers, and left, awkward at an event where they weren't supposed to be the center of attention, touching in their sorrow for Avery.

I started to disintegrate. I shouldn't have drunk that beer so fast. I should have had an aspirin. I couldn't remember if I'd brought my camera into the house with me. I bumped my way through the crowd, desperate to leave, searching for my jacket.

Marianne was standing by the kitchen door, a two-year-old boy in pajamas clutching her pant leg. She handed me my jacket, then lifted the child to her hip.

As I moved out the door, she said softly, "Remember to check about Lucas."

It was dark out, and the wind scuttled the dead leaves around my feet as I opened the truck door. The rain accentuated the rich, rotten, heavy scents of autumn. I turned the radio on to a golden oldies station and cried all the way back to the motel. I wanted my mother. And my father. And Avery.

4

I dreamed I was in a boat, an aluminum rowboat, with Avery and Grandad. Avery and I were fishing with bamboo poles, and we were using those red-and-white plastic bobbers that look like Ping-Pong balls with stems. Then something took my hook and dragged the bobber under the surface. A shock of tension ran up my pole. It was a big one, all right—maybe a bass. It yanked hard at the line, and then again, harder. Avery started yelling. Whatever it was was so strong I had to stand up to keep the pole under control. Avery was trying to help me, but Grandad kept yelling at him to let me do it myself. I was pulling with all my strength, and now Grandad was yelling too; yelling because the water started to swirl and we were in a whirlpool and I was still holding on to the pole and we were spinning in the boat, we were in orbit around this thing at the end of my line—

I sat upright in the bed, then sank back. A sliver of blue neon light from the sign in the parking lot shone through the space where the drapes didn't meet, lighting up the corner of the bureau and the TV. I pulled the bedspread, some sort of quilted, slippery, polyester stuff with flowers the size of hubcaps printed on it, up to my shoulders.

God, I hadn't had a dream that scary or real in years.

Grandad had been wearing green hip boots; Avery had on a
baseball jacket. I could still hear their voices and the sound
of the water.

I walked across the room for a glass of water, still breathing hard, still scared. It was raining again, and I could hear
the drops pinging against the cars parked just outside the
door and the steady gush of water through a drainpipe near
my window.

When I lived with Hugh I used to tell him my dreams in
the morning, while he looked for his socks and I tried to
muster the energy to get out of bed. Sometimes now I told
them to Claire, but she was never really interested unless
they had sex in them.

It was four-thirty. I wished I still smoked. I hit every button on the remote control and saw six test patterns. The public
station played Debussy and fixed its camera on a tank of
fish. I turned the thing off and lay back in bed. My head
banged against a section of mattress that had worn so thin I
could touch the bed frame's supporting slats through it. The
Mattress from Hell, I thought, palpating its lumps with my
hand. It Moves; It Speaks; It Carries Unspeakable Diseases.

I squirmed until I found an accommodating depression,
and bunched the pillow under my face.

I had to call that lawyer in the morning and set up an
appointment with him. And I had to go to Avery's school.
What did Marianne Dallas say about the dog? Would I have
to figure out what to do with it? Marianne hadn't looked so
hot, either. She looked like she did diet pills. Or worried a
lot. Or maybe both. What a neurotic! And I thought they
only lived in New York.

When I woke up again the rain had stopped. I yanked on
the same outfit I'd worn the day before—black corduroy skirt,
gray turtleneck sweater, black leather jacket, and a yellow
silk scarf with flowers on it. I had a black turtleneck and a

pair of blue jeans in my bag. My uniform for moving fast and light. What was that Muhammad Ali line? "Float like a butterfly, sting like a bee."

A sign taped to the mirror in the bathroom said *Complimentary coffee in lounge.* The offer sounded good; I could drink my coffee and read the paper in a nice, fat chair while I pulled today's agenda together. I hung my camera around my neck and walked across the parking lot, stopping to take a picture of the motel sign—the words ARROWHEAD MOTEL, *Sleep Like a Rock* surrounded by a huge neon outline of an arrowhead that glowed gently against the overcast sky. My neck and shoulders ached as I moved my head and arms to frame the shot. More like sleep *on* a rock, I thought.

I crossed the parking lot and studied the building next door—a long, low, windowless building, freshly painted white. A huge white half-circle of wood, or maybe metal, rose over the horizon of the building's roofline. Six-foot-tall letters, enameled deep blue and spelling out ROLLERCADE, radiated from the rim. The front doors were massive and padlocked. I shot half a roll of film from the Arrowhead parking lot as the light on the building and the clouds behind it shifted; then I walked out to the middle of the road in front of the Rollercade and took a few more shots dead-on. It looked regal and pristine, like an ocean liner, or a mammoth bank of fresh snow, against the pale-gray sky. Might be a keeper, I thought.

I used up the rest of the roll taking pictures of the Arrowhead, then went to the lounge, which was an alcove next to the office where I'd checked in for my room. It had two plastic-webbed aluminum lawn chairs and a card table with a wastebasket-sized coffeemaker on it. The only newspaper was a day-old *USA Today* jammed under the front legs of the coffeemaker to soak up the drips. I tilted the machine so the last ounce of coffee oozed into my cup in a gritty stream, and extracted a jelly-filled doughnut from a white cardboard box.

The room was dim, and the light from a desktop black-

and-white TV illuminated the clerk's face. She had a hairdo
the size of a cookie jar, and artificial fingernails painted copper. She pretended to watch a talk show, but she was really
watching me. Whenever I looked up, her head swung back
to the tube. The exertion had caused dark strands of hair to
escape from her wig at the nape of her neck. Diane Arbus
would have thought she'd hit pay dirt.

Training her eyes on the screen, she said, "Them dough-
nuts are thirty-five cents apiece."

I decided not to sit in the lounge, left a quarter and a dime
on the counter, and headed out to the parking lot.

The route to the high school was vaguely familiar. I had a
bleary recollection of driving in this direction with my mother
and Avery in the autumn, for apples maybe. Somewhere
where there was a big cider press they let you watch. How
old would I have been? Seven? Eight?

The air was cool and sharp and stung my nostrils. I opened
the window, jutted my elbow out, and breathed long and
deep. My eyes were still sensitive from my crying jag the
night before, and I welcomed the fresh air against my cheeks.

I love this kind of driving. Not another car in sight—just
a cool gray expanse of road curving off to the horizon, fringed
here and there with a row of poplars leading to a farmhouse
and a barn, or a loose gathering of cows. Not at all like Manhattan driving. My Rabbit, the victim of eight years of parallel parking and at least as many break-ins, looks like it
survived reentry from outer space. Last time they stole my
rubber floor mats and my sun visors.

So Avery took this drive every day. He must have memo-
rized every tree, every barn, every utility pole. He must have
seen that big lake over by the Christmas tree farm freeze and
thaw a dozen times.

I turned on the radio. The station that carried golden oldies the night before now offered a call-in show. They were talking about recipes. About how to sprinkle confectioner's sugar through a doily to make a pattern on gingerbread. I turned it off.

For someone who'd been such a messy child, Avery kept his truck immaculate. No disemboweled road maps on the floor, no wads of paper towels, no candy bar wrappers. Just a neatly folded brown wool blanket on the passenger seat, a pair of aviator sunglasses tucked into a slot above the heater knobs, and a plastic travel mug mounted on the dash. The mug was half full of cold coffee. It gave me a chill. I pulled over and chucked the contents out the window.

I checked the map Vince Scannell had drawn for me, and turned right at the Sohio station at the intersection of Route 12 and Route 221. Marshall County Regional High School loomed in the distance, windowless, grim, blocklike, and as big as a shopping mall. I left the truck in Visitor Parking and headed for the tinted-glass front doors.

Classes were in session. I managed to make out a sign that said ADMINISTRATIVE OFFICES at the far left end of the entry corridor and walked toward it, my footsteps barking on the polyurethaned concrete. The hall was lit by an expanse of fluorescent lights, some dimmer than others, a few pulsating in those death throes peculiar to fluorescent lights. It reminded me of the way they build the big Las Vegas casinos without windows—to erase the distinction between night and day and keep the customers concentrating on the games.

Vince Scannell was handing some papers to his secretary. "You're in luck," he said. "Third period just started, and there's no class in Avery's room. You can clear the place out in peace."

He took me up a stairway draped with a huge banner that said BLAST 'EM BULLDOGS!

"It's been tough on Avery's students," he said. "A lot of kids really looked up to him. Suicide—we haven't had one of those around this school for five, six years."

He was the kind of person who didn't expect you to re-

spond, or wouldn't listen if you did, so I let him do all the
talking.

"We arranged for some counseling, and had the minister
in a couple of times, but it's hard on the kids. Suicide, that
is. Plus we have to get a new teacher."

Was I supposed to apologize?

Avery's classroom looked like every science classroom I'd
ever been in. A big counter with a sink at the head of the
class, thirty or so metal-and-yellow-wood chairs with arm-
rest writing areas, a lab area at the back, with more sinks.
Someone, maybe Avery, had drawn an elaborate chart of the
life cycle of the fern on the blackboard in yellow chalk.

Avery's desk sat in a narrow office and lab preparation area
off the front of the classroom.

Scannell motioned toward the desk, then headed for the
door. "Everything in the desk, on the bulletin board, and on
those shelves is Avery's. I'll have one of the kids bring you a
box."

"Including the computer?"

He pointed at a gray box.

"Just the disk drive. Avery used it to convert the disks he
used at home to the right size for the school computers."

"The picture?"

I was looking at a framed print of a turtle hanging over
Avery's desk.

"No, that belongs to the school."

Scannell disappeared down the hall, and I turned to my
task. Why did I have to do this? Why didn't Scannell do it
himself? Why didn't one of Avery's teacher friends, if they
were so desperate to be useful?

I started with the desk. The top was covered with a sheet
of glass, which lay over an orderly arrangement of snapshots
and postcards. Avery standing next to a hibachi, in a chef's
hat, pretending to jab a dark-haired guy with a barbecue
fork. Avery and a woman on a sofa. Lots of fishing pictures—
of Avery standing on a dock somewhere, dangling a catfish
from the line in its mouth; Avery in a rowboat with a man

with a yellow beard; Avery with a yellow dog that must be Lucas, loading fishing poles into the back of the pickup; Avery at a kitchen table with Ted Dallas, holding up a trout on a plate, a huge grin on his face. There were pictures of students at science fairs, and pictures of a trip out West. There was a color snapshot with wide white borders of my mother and grandfather sitting on the glider on the porch at Grandad's, shucking corn, and another picture that Grandad must have taken the same day of Avery, Mom, and me sitting on the back steps, eating the corn. My eyes filled up, and I made an untidy stack of the photos and another of the postcards.

The desk drawers were practically bare. Someone had already taken any teaching materials or grade books. Some pencils, a squashed box of Kleenex, a ChapStick, a roll of butter-rum Life Savers in one drawer; a couple of back issues of *Scientific American* in another.

A girl in overalls came into the office with a cardboard box. "Mr. Scannell says you want this."

I thanked her and started filling it up.

Some reference books, a box of glass slides, and a small trophy inscribed *M.C.R.H.S. 1980 Teacher of the Year.* A travel umbrella, a soup thermos, and a digital clock.

I picked up the disk drive. There was a yellowed IBM brochure underneath it, a chewed-up pencil, and a computer disk in a protective envelope with *Royalco* written on the label in Avery's handwriting. I wedged everything into the box.

I was almost finished when a boy came into the room and started rinsing out the petri dishes stacked in the sink.

"Are you taking Mr. Kincaid's things?"

He was thin and small, with brown eyes and dirty-blond hair, and he wore brown jeans and high-top sneakers. His voice was high and wobbly. I put him at about fourteen, but I'm no judge of children's ages.

"Yeah. Somebody has to."

He folded his arms across his chest, more like hugging himself than a belligerent gesture.

"I saw you at the funeral. Are you his sister?"

I started to extend my hand for a handshake, but drew it back when he didn't respond. I forgot—that's what you do when you meet an editor, not a teenager.

"Yes, I'm Libby Kincaid. And I'm supposed to take care of things for him now that he's dead."

It was the wrong thing to say. I don't know what the right thing to say was, but that was the wrong thing. The boy started sniffling and wiping at his nose with the back of his hand.

He spoke first.

"He was my best friend. I told him everything. We did all kinds of things together. I did his lab work for him."

He had stopped sniffling, but he had to take a gulp of air between every sentence. I asked him his name.

"Kevin Kogut," he said. "Ted Dallas is my stepfather. The famous coach Ted Dallas. He wants to adopt me, but I won't let him. He was friends with Avery too."

God, he looked like Marianne. So this was who Ted had asked about in the kitchen. The kid who took off on his bike after the funeral.

He looked down at his sneakers while he talked. "I keep thinking he must have left a note. He wouldn't not say good-bye. Not Avery."

"I don't think there's a note, Kevin. I wish he'd left one too."

"If he was feeling bad he should have told me. I told him when I felt bad. I told him everything. I would have helped him. Who am I going to talk to now?"

Jeez, the boy was feeling responsible for Avery's death. Just like me, I suppose, and just like Avery's teacher friends. If only we'd known . . . if only he'd come to us for help . . .

I sat down in the chair at Avery's desk.

"Look, Kevin, there are plenty of people you can talk to about this. There's your mom, and there's Ted, and—"

"I can't talk to Ted about anything. Right, he talks. Talks all the time. Talks, talks, talks—about nothing. Be a good sport. Keep your chin up. Think positive. Don't be a baby. No excuses, just results. He's full of shit, and I hate him. I don't know why my mom married him. Don't tell me to talk to him—"

His voice grew higher and higher, then broke again. I tried another tack to calm him down.

"Kevin, what kind of projects did you work on with Avery?"

"I did some lab work for him when he finished up his thesis last summer. On pigmentation in newts. And I kind of helped him prepare for class. You know, got the equipment ready, made sure everything in the lab was clean. He was starting a new project too. About mayflies. He was all excited about that and said I could help him. He said we might even be able to use the electron microscope at the university. And he said he was going to help me work out a project for the Westinghouse contest next year."

"Well, don't you think it would be a good idea to get going on a project now? Even though Avery's not here? Can't you get another teacher to work with you?"

It didn't work. The flush that had come over him while he talked about his work with Avery drained right out again. My specialty—saying the wrong thing.

"Nobody will be like Avery."

He turned back to the sink and started to rinse the petri dishes a second time. He was in misery.

I took the snapshot of Avery holding the catfish from the pile and put it next to the sink.

"Maybe you'd like to have this, Kevin."

He said nothing, and I left.

5

I was back on the road into Darby by eleven, Kevin Kogut weighing on my mind. Adolescents. How can anybody bear to be with them all day? All those hormones. All those conflicts and sensitivities. No wonder the county warehouses them in those huge windowless buildings and drives them from class to class with bells.

Avery taught them for what—twelve, thirteen years?

God knows at Kevin's age I wasn't any different—probably worse. I was living with my mother's sister and her husband in Rochester. It was too much for my grandfather to take care of Avery and me both after our mother died, and no one knew where my father was. Besides, Avery had only a year of high school left, so it made sense for him to finish up in Darby, but I was starting eighth grade. A perfect time for the change, everyone said. Uncle Garth worked at Eastman Kodak, and my aunt taught piano at home. They were good to me, considering I was the last thing they'd expected to land in their laps after the youngest of their three children had left for college.

Uncle Garth had a darkroom in the basement. By the time I was Keven Kogut's age I all but lived in it, wearing a headband and bell-bottom blue jeans, my transistor radio tuned to a local rock station. Uncle Garth encouraged my "interest," as he called it, bringing home mountains of photographic paper and chemicals on demand. I returned the favor by turning morose and stormy, smoking dope in the garage, and getting sent home from school for wearing my skirts too short. In another year I darkly condemned my aunt and uncle for being "establishment"; two years later I ran away to New York City for the summer and scared holy hell out of them.

I stopped for gas, vowing to remain childless forever.

I didn't want to go back to the Arrowhead in the middle of the day. Instead, I took a tour through Darby, to see if anything had stayed the same.

Not much had. I drove past Grandad's place on Anchor Road. Someone had started and stopped an aluminum siding job on the house. One side was the same old white clapboard; half the front and another side were pale-green aluminum strips. Pink insulation leaked out of the seam between the wood and the aluminum like bologna from a sandwich.

A car was parked in the front yard, its backside propped up on concrete blocks, the back window a spiderweb of cracks and electrical tape. The lawn was bald in spots, and the white wooden shed where Grandad used to put up his tomatoes and keep his gardening tools pitched crazily to the right.

I stood on the lawn and took a picture of the house for old times' sake, and one of the car for art's sake. Inside the house, a barking dog leapt at the front door, and I got back into Avery's truck.

The rest of the street looked pretty much as I remembered it, but smaller, of course, and there were two trailers in what used to be the empty lot at the corner.

I crossed the center of town. Isaly's Dairy Bar, where we used to get skyscraper cones, was gone, and so was the post office. There was a 7-Eleven where the bakery had been, and the movie theater was boarded shut. I took some pictures of a vintage Coca-Cola vending machine—the kind that dispen-

ses bottles, not cans—in front of a gas station, and some of
the handles on the front doors of the movie theater, which
were shaped like mermaids.

I wanted to see Avery's house; I'm not sure why. I'd thought
about him constantly for the last few days; maybe I thought
I'd make contact with him somehow if I saw his belongings,
his bed, whatever the last things were that he'd seen.

I'd never been there. The last time I'd been in Darby, three
years earlier—when I'd seen my father—Avery had been
renting the top floor of an old house downtown. He'd bought
this house a year or so ago and had sent me a picture of it. I
didn't know the number, but I knew the street name.

I stopped at the 7-Eleven and bought a Coke and a prefab
tuna sandwich in plastic wrap. I asked the clerk if he knew
where Garfield Road was.

"Sure do," he said. "Over by my sister's place. Where that
teacher shot himself last week. My sister thinks she heard
the gun, but you know my sister. Watches too much T.V."

He shook his head. "Tragic, though. A teacher. Imagine.
Just drive out Central and turn left after the overpass. After
that it's three, maybe four turns in on the left. I bet a lot of
folks have been driving by there this week, just to see the
place. I might drive the family over by there myself this
weekend."

"Imagine," I said. "A teacher."

I recognized Avery's place from the picture. A long driveway lined on one side with spruce trees, and then a small
brown one-story bungalow that had a screened-in side porch
and green shutters with pine-tree shapes punched out of them.
The nearest neighbor was a quarter of a mile away, on the
other side of an apple orchard.

There was a green plastic mat at the front door, heaped
up with newspapers and campaign fliers and something from

the Jehovah's Witnesses. I nudged it all aside with my foot
and tried the keys on the ring that had come with Avery's
pickup. None of them worked.

I went around to the back door. It swung open at my touch.
Dumb cops, I thought. Anybody could come clean the place
out.

It was Avery's, all right. There were hip boots in the back
hall and a fishing vest, flannel shirt, and rain poncho hanging from a hook beside them. The sight of them made my
heart tighten. I walked through the hall and into the living
room, glancing at but not entering the kitchen. I half expected, or maybe wanted, to see him sitting there at the dinette, drinking a cup of coffee.

The house was stuffy and a little dark. I set the box of
Avery's school things on the floor, pulled up the living room
shades, opened a window, and sat on the sofa.

The room was nice. Nicer than I would have expected. Just
because he was my brother was he supposed to live like me—
mattress on the floor, a trunk with a board over it for a table, photographic equipment heaped in the corner, and piles
of books everywhere?

He'd painted the walls beige and off-white. The mantel was
clear except for a black Indian pot with a brown band around
the center. Next to the fireplace he had two heavy, mission-
style chairs with Navajo blankets draped over their backs,
and along one wall there was a long, low bookcase, hardcov-
ers on one shelf, paperbacks on the other, their spines exactly flush with one another. Lots of science books—maybe
textbooks from graduate school—then a section of art books,
then a long section of books about American Indians. He'd
made low, tidy stacks of magazines on top of the bookcase.
About a year's worth of *Smithsonians*, *Scientific Americans*,
and *Ohio Magazines*.

How could I have known so little about my own brother?

What happened? Why hadn't we connected more? A four-
year age difference was a pretty lame excuse. He wrote me;

I took months to write back, and sometimes I never answered. He called me—always on my birthday, always on
Christmas, every once in a while in the middle of the night
on no occasion at all. For a while he used to invite me out
to Ohio—for Thanksgiving, for Memorial Day weekend. I always had something else to do. Or I was going to Vermont
with Hugh. Or I just didn't want to go. After a while he didn't
call so often.

What was wrong with me?

I remembered Avery's room at Grandad's, crammed with
model airplanes, dirty clothes, horned toads, and back issues
of *Popular Science.* I ran the back of my hand along the top
row of books. But here, I thought, a place for everything,
everything in its—

The pump in the aquarium on the stand next to the fireplace made a gurgling sound, and I nearly jumped out of my
skin. Too much coffee, I thought. Too much Coke.

I walked over to the tank. All belly-up, no doubt, I thought.
All starved to death.

No, the tank was crystal clear and full of living fish—tetra
blues, skeleton fish, gouramis—some of them darting to the
surface and dragging down flecks of what looked like brown
fish food. Weird, I thought. Where'd they get that food? I
picked up a small cardboard box with a picture of a fish on
it that was next to the tank.

At the same time I heard footsteps coming up the basement steps and into the kitchen. Silence, then the refrigerator door opening and closing. I froze for a moment, then
walked into the hall.

"Hello—who's there?"

No answer. I thought about making a run for the truck.
But whoever it was would hear me open the front door, and
if I went for the back door I'd have to pass by the kitchen. I
tried again.

"Hey—who is it?"

A dark-haired, wide-shouldered man about five foot ten, in

hunting boots and a green-and-black plaid jacket, stepped into the hall. He had a bottle of Rolling Rock in one hand, and he looked at me like I was a bug from Mars.

"Dan Sikora," he said. "Who the hell are you?"

Where had I seen him before?

I hung back in the doorway, hoping I looked steely-eyed.

"Libby. I'm Libby Kincaid. Avery's sister. What are you doing here?"

He opened the refrigerator, took out another beer, and twisted off the cap with part of his sleeve. He held the bottle out to me.

"Seems like that's the kind of question I should be asking you."

I took the beer and stepped into the kitchen.

"Are you a friend of Avery's?"

"I guess you could say that."

"I didn't see you at the funeral."

He held the back of his arm up to his eyes, feigning defense.

"Whoa there. Attack mode, huh?"

"Thanks for the beer and all, but for all I know, you could be a serial killer escaped from the Mansfield Penitentiary."

He sat down at the dinette and leaned back in his chair.

"For chrissake," he said. "I was just feeding the fish."

I was still trying to place where I'd seen him before. Then I remembered—those snapshots of Avery's from his desk at school. He looked like the guy in the hibachi picture.

I relaxed a little.

"Okay," he said. "How's this? Your real name is Olivia. You lived in Darby when you were a kid, then you lived with your relatives in upstate New York, and you went to school at the Rochester Institute of Technology. You moved to New York eight or nine years ago, and you run around the country taking pictures for magazines. You won a prize a couple of years ago for taking a picture of teenage fathers in Harlem or someplace. You had a boyfriend for a long time, but he jerked you around. You used to wear your hair real long, then you went sort of punk. Your brother thought you were real hot shit."

I suddenly felt like I hadn't slept for a week.

"How do you know all this?"

He looked me full in the face.

"Either I'm a psychic or your brother and I were real good buddies."

I sat down in the chair at the other side of the table.

"You're right," I said. "Sorry. I'm a little on edge."

"Fine," he said. "Me, too. You scared the pants off me when you came in here."

He wasn't conventionally handsome, but he had a broad, appealing face. His eyebrows were heavy and met in the middle, and his cheeks were very pink. He had longish thick brown hair and a bad haircut. Self-inflicted, I supposed.

I looked at his hunting boots.

"Are you a hunter?"

He seemed to think this was funny.

"Hell, no. I don't even fish. Can't stand to kill the worms."

"Then why the boots?"

"I like them," he said. "They're warm."

I couldn't understand why I was talking such drivel. Who cared about his boots?

Then I realized that I wasn't just sad about Avery; I was lonely. I'd been talking with strangers for two days. I hadn't been in Darby much since I was a kid, but every time I'd been there, Avery had been too. Now I was a stranger in town.

I kept it up.

"Do you live around here?"

He squinted at the print on the beer bottle.

"I've got a little junk and antique place on Central Street. I live in the upstairs."

"Do you have any old photos?"

"Some," he said. "Mostly *cartes de visite* and old photo

cards. And some stuff that I don't sell, if you want to see that."

"Are you open this afternoon? I could use some distraction."

"Sure," he said, and looked at his watch. "In fact, I've got to be getting back now. I told somebody I'd meet him at one."

I needed to stay a little longer at Avery's; I don't know why.

"I'll come by later. Where on Central?"

"Right after the bridge. In the little flatiron building where Central crosses Erie. You'll see it."

He zipped up his jacket and took a reddish-brown envelope off the kitchen counter and put it under his arm. It was one of those big accordion-pleated ones that you close by winding the string around the clasp, and it had a large black stain near the bottom of the front, as though someone had left a Magic Marker without a cap on top of it.

He paused for a moment, dug in his pocket, and handed me a key.

"It's to the front door," he said. "I guess there's no need for me to keep it anymore. You can take care of the fish."

I went back in the living room and watched him walk down the driveway to his van, parked across the road. It was dark blue, dirty, and the open sliding door was black. I felt drowsy from the beer, so I wrapped myself in one of the Indian blankets and lay on the couch for a while, flipping through magazines and watching the fish. My eyes landed on a red plaid dog bed crammed in a corner of the room next to the bookcase. Lucas's bed. Who would take care of him now?

I went into the kitchen and found "Pam Bates, V.M.D." in the phone directory. Her receptionist told me she was "in surgery" and that she could call me back in ten minutes. I put the kettle on for some coffee and went into Avery's bedroom, a small, dark room with a platform bed, a chest of drawers, a framed "Save the Turtles" poster, and a desk rigged from a sawhorse and a two-drawer file cabinet. The desk's surface was clear except for a jar of pencils, a calendar, and a computer monitor and keyboard. I ran my finger across the tops of the folders in the file cabinet. Avery must have kept every paper and every bit of research he'd done since high school. Each folder was marked by a narrow typed label, and they all seemed to be organized in some sort of color-coded system.

The disk drive was under the desk, along with a small plastic box meant to contain disks—the kind Hugh used to store his disks in. I opened the box and flipped through the disks. The first one was labeled *Thesis 1*. Behind it were *Thesis 2*, *Thesis 3*, and *Misc.*

I slipped the first disk into the disk drive and found the beginning of the text. "The Control of Pigment Cell Pattern Formation in *Notopthalmus viridescens*," it said, and then, in a block of type a few inches below the title, "Avery Parker Kincaid, Ohio University," and "Alison Linden, Ph.D., Robert Pfeiffer, Ph.D., and C. L. Heaver, Ph.D."—his faculty advisers, I supposed. Then he launched into a Byzantine description of how a newt could turn itself green by pumping up its black, yellow, and silver cells.

I remembered the disk that I'd found in Avery's office—the one labeled *Royalco*—got it from the box of Avery's school things, and inserted it into the computer. The only document in the index was titled "Jarvis Beck." The name of a student? A colleague?

I pulled the document up. It was a chart with columns across the top labeled "pH," "Halogenated Aliphatic Hydrocarbons," and "Substituted Benzenes," and a vertical axis with dates, and it meant nothing to me. I took it out and replaced it with the disk labeled *Misc.* The document index was perfectly clear: "Three-Alarm Chili," "Guacamole," "Marianne Dallas's Bar-B-Q Sauce," and some thirty or forty other items. For the first time in days I laughed out loud. Most people can't get organized enough to keep all their recipes together in one shoe box; Avery kept his on disk.

God, he was a sweet brother, I thought. I remembered him

making our sandwiches for school, cutting the crusts off mine, wrapping everything up in immaculate wax-paper packages. My chin trembled and my eyes grew misty. This is going to be hard, I thought—sorting through Avery's things, remembering when we were a family.

The last document listed in the index was titled simply "Note." Next to "Date created" it said "10/26," the date of Avery's death. I brought the document up. Except for information about how many blocks had been used and how many remained on the disk, the screen was empty. What had he planned to write? A lecture note for class?

Unfinished business, I thought. Too much unfinished business. I returned to the document index. Next to "Date created: 10/26," it said "Time elapsed: 04:26." He must have gotten distracted, I thought, and forgotten to turn the machine off.

The phone rang while I was placing the disks back in their box. The voice on the other end was young but husky-sounding, and tinged with a southern drawl.

"This is Dr. Bates," she said. "You called me."

"Hello," I said. "I'm Avery Kincaid's sister, and I understand you're taking care of his dog."

"That's right."

"I was hoping I could come by and see him, and talk with you about what to do with him. I live in New York, and I've never had a dog . . ."

"And you want one that's half dead?"

"I suppose that's part of the problem, but I'm not sure that I want one at all."

"Look, Avery Kincaid's sister," she said. "I'm taking care of this dog because there's nobody else around who can do it. But as soon as he's better—that's if he gets better—I'm finding somebody to give him to. If you want to see him, you can come around tomorrow."

"How do I get to your place?"

"If you figured out my phone number, you can figure that out too."

Emotional age seventeen, I noted.

"Thanks for taking care of Lucas."

But she'd hung up.

I made a cup of instant coffee and sat back down on the sofa. Through the front window I could see a station wagon move slowly down the road past the apple orchard, followed a moment later by two boys on bicycles. The spruce trees that lined Avery's driveway cast long spade-shaped shadows on the lawn.

The sky was growing overcast, and suddenly the house felt very cold.

6

Dan Sikora's shop was a minute iron-shaped building perched on a triangular lot formed by the intersection of Central Street and Erie Road—the same idea as the Flatiron Building in New York at Broadway and Fifth Avenue. But while the twenty-one-story Flatiron's acute angles and ornate stone-work sail with confidence over Madison Square Park, Sikora's building, a squat three floors of narrow red brick, looked more like a tiny stranded tugboat. Like the other buildings on the block, it seemed to sag a little, as though a huge invisible hand were pressing on it from above.

I parked in front of a broken meter and crossed the road to the store's entrance on Central Street. The building didn't have an outdoor sign, but TIME TRAVEL was lettered in black and gold on the front door. An orange-and-white cardboard OPEN sign was propped up in the front window by an enormous old work boot. The rest of the window was filled with hands—a row of big white porcelain ones that I guessed were lasts for glovemaking, a dozen or so hand-shaped brass door knockers, and a few small ceramic hands in yellows and blacks, palm up, that served as shallow dishes. One held a heart-shaped locket, opened to show an old photograph of a woman with a bow in her hair; another cupped a minuscule pair of dice. Everything looked dusty, which somehow enhanced the surreal effect of the display.

A fat man in a tight safari jacket left the shop as I entered. He looked back to have a last word with Sikora, who was sitting behind a glass display box at the back of the store.

"You don't know what you're missing! Somebody's going to make a fortune off this!"

Sikora was prying some nails from the back of an old picture frame. He didn't look up.

"I know, I know. I'll regret it for the rest of my life."

Sikora saw me.

"Well, shucks, ma'am. I didn't hear you come in."

I sat on a piano stool that sank to the right under my weight.

"What was he trying to sell you?"

"Pictures of Chinese women with bound feet. He says it's the best collection there is."

"Sounds like it might be valuable."

"He cut them out of an old *Life* magazine."

"I see."

The triangular room was about twelve feet across at its widest point and narrowed dramatically to its apex at the back, where Sikora sat. He had looked like an average-sized man at Avery's, but here he looked like a linebacker for the New York Giants.

Looking at the store was like looking at those elaborate drawings that they used to put in children's magazines with captions like "Can you find the hammer in this picture?" Every inch of wall space was covered—with old photographs, paper fans, calendars, posters, and display frames full of campaign buttons. Next to the stool I was sitting on was a wooden table crammed with old calling cards, paperweights, and bookends; in the center there was a stuffed fox, standing upright and wearing a vest and a red-and-white-striped bow tie. He held a coaster-sized tray in an outstretched paw, and the tray held a small stack of business cards. *Time Travel,* they said, and under that: *T. Daniel Sikora, Labor and Union Photographs, Photographic Postcards, Paper Ephemera.*

A two-foot-long panoramic photograph of what looked like a family reunion hung on the wall behind Sikora, who was still concentrating on extracting the nails from the picture frame. Above the photograph there was a shelf of Mason jars filled with marbles. The light coming in through a narrow, dusty window on the side wall threw the colors of the marbles in a patch against the floor like a small, iridescent rug. Too bad I'd just loaded my camera with black-and-white film.

"I keep my labor collection upstairs," said Sikora. "I only have a couple of steady customers around here for them; the rest of the time I deal them at shows."

I opened a drawer in a postcard cabinet and began to look through the photo cards—a nice selection of turn-of-the-century studio portraits of people sitting on plywood crescent moons and meteors or in make-believe boats shooting through make-believe rapids.

Sikora looked over at me.

"Avery used to like photo cards," he said. "Especially the ones of people holding fish. I was saving some for him."

He reached into a box near his feet, pulled out a handful of cards, and placed them slowly and carefully in a row on the counter, like someone setting up a solitaire game. One was of a man in a straw hat standing in a rowboat, showing off a snapping turtle by hanging it from a stick held in its mouth; another was a faded picture of a disheveled-looking woman in a white dress dangling a weird-looking fish the size and shape of a baseball bat from a bit of line held in her hand.

"The image isn't so good," said Sikora, "but it's got a great message." I read: *Dear Irene, Ain't this a grand fish? It fought like a cat but I got it good. Lizzie.*

The others were more mundane but somehow just as appealing: a young boy with a sunfish that fit in the palm of his hand, a man with his face completely obscured by the fish he held up, a bare-chested teenager in white trousers holding a sailfish by its snout against a backdrop of heavy surf.

Sikora gathered the cards and held them out to me.

"Do you like them?"

"Of course I do. They're wonderful."

"Take them."

I have a perverse, unexplainable inclination to refuse gifts, but Sikora sounded so sincere that I couldn't turn him down. Besides, I really did like the pictures. I slid them into the back pocket of my camera bag.

"Do you want a cup of coffee?"

This was what—my fourth cup today?

"Sure."

He stepped sideways into a tiny alcove partitioned from the cash register area by a yellow shower curtain and poured water into a saucepan from a sink the size of a mixing bowl.

"What's the 'T' for?"

"You want tea?"

I hollered at him over the water.

"No! The 'T' in 'T. Daniel Sikora.' "

He lit the gas flame on a decrepit single burner with a twisted-up piece of newspaper, balanced the saucepan on top, and took two coffee mugs that said OHIO TURNPIKE from beneath the sink.

No response.

"I said, what's the 'T' in 'T. Daniel Sikora' for?"

He shoveled some damp coffee grounds from a soup can into the saucepan. My flesh crawled.

"I heard you." He was searching for something in another cardboard box on the floor. "Theodore," he said. "But maybe Thomas."

"What do you mean—*maybe* Thomas?"

He was still rifling the box.

"And sometimes I think maybe Tyrone."

"What are you talking about—maybe Thomas, maybe Tyrone?"

"The initial. I made it up. I was having the cards printed up, and I thought, Well, what the hell, let's make it 'T.' Daniel Sikora. Writers do it all the time."

"Are you a writer?"

"Are you kidding?" He stood up. "I can't find any creamer. Look around the shop some more, and I'll go down to the 7-Eleven and get some."

"Do you mind if I take some pictures?"

"Go ahead. But give me some prints. How's that?"

I lifted my Leica and trapped the stuffed fox in my lens. His glass eyes had acquired a malevolent-looking glare in the afternoon sun.

"Sure," I said, "if anything's worth printing."

Most people who don't take photographs for a living seem to think that you print every last picture that you take, which couldn't be further from the truth. I usually end up printing five or six images from a roll of film and throwing out most of the prints. It used to drive Hugh crazy. Once I found him picking through my darkroom trash. "I don't get you," he said, holding up a dented wad of prints. "These are perfectly good. You could *sell* these." I guess Claire was right: Hugh and I were about as compatible as charcoal and lighter fluid.

Sikora yanked on his jacket and disappeared down the street.

The shower curtain by the kitchen had taken on a soft luminescence from the light coming through the window over the sink. I spread it open a little further and shot it five or six times, then squeezed myself into the kitchen to try and get a view toward the front of the store. No good. I surveyed the kitchen. The coffee grounds stewing in the saucepan looked foul but smelled like coffee. I wondered where Sikora had picked up his brewing method: Outward Bound? The army? A chain gang?

On the wall above the hot plate hung a bulletin board shingled with cut-out newspaper articles, postcards, snapshots, and a 1933 Dionne Quintuplets wall calendar. One snapshot was of a three- or four-year-old boy who looked like he might be Sikora standing next to a giant ball of string. The others were more recent, including a duplicate print of the photograph of Sikora and Avery that I'd found at the high school. The postcards were weird, lurid cards from the forties, most with Florida themes. One, of a woman in an evening gown reclining on a pile of fruit, was titled "A Florida Blossom Among Grapefruit and Oranges"; another, of a little girl riding on the back of an alligator, said "Four on the Floor in the Sunshine State."

I walked out to the sidewalk and took some pictures of the front door, the black-and-gold lettering lambent in the late-afternoon sun. Then I backed into the street and took a few shots of the window display. The way the long white porcelain hands rising from the black cloth looked at that distance reminded me of something sad from a Stevie Smith poem, something about waving and drowning, but I couldn't remember what it was.

I crossed the street and focused on the entire storefront as Sikora returned with a paper bag in his hand. He went into the store, and I took some more pictures; then he reappeared in the doorway and looked down the street—for me, I guessed.

"Hey," I hollered. "Over here!"

He looked, and I squeezed the shutter.

He scowled and stepped backward into the store. I waited for a car to pass and followed him in.

"I thought you cut out on me," he said. "That you didn't like the company or something."

"Not at all. I just liked how the front of the store looked in the light."

He poured the coffee into the mugs, damming the grounds back in the saucepan with the edge of a spoon.

I liked watching Sikora use his hands. They were large and very square, and he moved them slowly, gently, and with great precision. I set my camera on his desk, and he handed me my mug.

"Are you from around here?" I asked him. "I don't remember any Sikoras when we were kids."

Sikora squeezed back into the kitchen with the saucepan, then reappeared.

"No, I'm not from around here," he said. "I lived in Arizona from when I was born until I joined the service. My folks are still there, in the same house."

"How long have you had the shop?"

He spooned some creamer into his coffee and looked down a list of numbers on a yellow pad of paper. I felt as though I were talking on a bad long-distance phone connection—the kind where there's an extended pause before your voice is received by the other side, and you wonder if you should repeat the question.

He kept his eyes on the yellow pad.

"I've been here about six years."

"How did you meet Avery?"

More silence. He set the yellow pad aside and took a long drag at his coffee. I sucked at mine too. It tasted like something leaked from a dead battery.

Sikora wasn't meeting my eyes. In fact, he had seemed determined not to look me in the face ever since I reentered the shop. Now he was flipping through a pile of what looked like invoices.

"Avery was one of my first customers. He was living in town then, over by the VFW hall. I sold him a file cabinet and some old baseball cards. Then he started stopping by here on Saturday afternoons, after he'd been fishing. We'd sit around and shoot the bull. Sometimes I'd close up shop and we'd go out for a beer. While he was seeing Pam we didn't get together so much."

His voice was deep but very soft. He looked at me as though he were about to say something else, but he seemed to reconsider. It was getting dark outside fast, and the outlines of everything in the store, including Sikora, had begun to go gray and dull.

"Pam Bates? The vet?"

"Yeah, Pam. They were together two, maybe three years."

He looked uneasy. I wondered if maybe he was the reason Avery and Pam had broken up. I decided to be direct.

"What was going on with them? Avery wouldn't tell me why they broke up. When he called me in August he just said that it didn't work out and he was taking it harder than he thought he should. But she didn't come to Avery's funeral, and when I talked with her on the phone about Lucas I got the feeling that if she could have, she'd have bitten my head off. What's the story?"

Sikora sat silently for a long moment, then leaned back in his chair, stretching out his legs in front of him.

"I suppose you have a right to know," he said. "Anyway, it's never been anybody's secret. Avery and Pam got really tight really fast. She has an apartment in town, but she spent most of her time at Avery's place. Last Christmas they were talking about moving in together permanently—maybe buying a house together near Pam's clinic. They seemed like a pretty good pair. Did you ever meet her?"

I was embarrassed, but I hadn't.

"Pam's pretty much of a character. She's gruff; I guess some people think she's pretty rude. But from what Avery told me, she's been through some tough times. She was married real young to some guy who roughed her up, went through a bad divorce, and put herself through college and vet school. She takes a long time to get to know, but once you do know her, you realize that she's pretty great. She's got a wicked sense of humor, and she'd do anything for an animal. Once I brought her a skunk that got his head stuck in a bottle. She didn't flinch; just knocked it out with a shot and pulled it out. Not before it stunk her and her office up pretty bad, though."

He laughed, and I got the feeling that I might have been on the right track when I wondered if she'd left Avery for him. Even if she hadn't, it seemed as though Sikora had a soft place for Pam Bates—as though things might have been different if he'd met her before Avery had.

So what he said next took me by surprise.

"Pam was pretty upset when she found out that Avery had been fooling around behind her back with a secretary from the high school. To tell you the truth, I was pretty mad myself. Pam was crazy about Avery; it was a rotten trick to pull on her."

I remembered the dark-haired woman who approached me at Ted Dallas's. The one who said they'd "dated for a while."

"When did this happen?"

"Who knows? He was probably seeing this other woman for most of the summer. Pam didn't find out until September. She saw them together at a restaurant up in Salem. She was furious. Avery said she screamed at him in the restaurant and the management threatened to call the cops. Then they had a big fight back at Avery's, and it was all over. She stopped talking to me for a while too. Guilt by association, I guess."

"She sounds like she has a temper."

"Maybe. But you can't blame her for being pissed at Avery."

"Marianne Dallas thinks Pam might have been mad enough at Avery to kill him."

Sikora brought the front legs of his chair back to earth.

"Look," he said, "I'd be the first person to say that there's something that isn't right about this idea that Avery killed himself. I knew him as well as anybody—in some ways, probably better than you did. And I know that he wasn't depressed, and that he had a lot of plans for the future. I've been trying to figure this out all week. But I know one thing absolutely, and that's that Pam Bates might have a temper but she'd never hurt a living creature—including a guy who jerked her over."

"How can you be so sure? You just told me they almost had to call the police because she screamed at him in a restaurant."

"I can be so sure because I was with Pam Bates at her house the night Avery died."

Score for the lady from Manhattan, I thought. Sikora really was involved with Pam Bates. Was this a coincidence, or had I finally acquired feminine intuition?

"Wait a minute," I said. "Do I have this straight? Avery was two-timing Pam Bates, but you and Pam Bates were two-timing Avery?"

"No," he said, "you don't have it straight. I went out with Pam a couple of times after she and Avery split up. It didn't work out. Now we see each other once in a while for a movie or dinner, but just as friends. I suppose it's more that we're both sort of lonely than anything else."

He looked uncomfortable. And why shouldn't he be? Most of his customers probably don't drill him for details about his love life.

"I'm sorry," I said. "Marianne Dallas seems a little bit on the neurotic side."

"That's okay," he said. "I've been kind of crazy myself all week. I'm having a hard time with the idea that Avery shot himself. Hey, the guy was happy. He came over here the day before he died. He was planning a trip down to Cape Hatteras at Thanksgiving. He was talking about starting some new research, and he asked me if I'd help him find some old maps. And he borrowed my power screwdriver because he said he was going to start building a shop in his basement. Does that sound like someone who was about to kill himself? And the split-up with Pam—that was over with a long time ago. I know he felt guilty, and he should have. Maybe it hit him harder than I realized. Maybe I should have talked to him more about it instead of chewing him out." He shook his head. "I just don't know."

The coffee was working on me. Sikora showed me to an outside staircase that led upstairs to his apartment, and I climbed up, alone, to use the bathroom.

His apartment looked like, and probably was, his warehouse. The main living area, triangle-shaped like the shop below, was wall-to-wall with storage cabinets, for photographs, I guessed. There was a dining room table stuffed into the center and a rickety kitchen off to one side. Another room angled out from the broad side of the room—an afterthought that hung over the parking area on stilts. It contained a desk heaped with boxes and manila envelopes, a double bed, a rubber plant that looked like it needed a leaf transplant, a circus poster advertising THE GREAT PETERS—THE MAN WITH THE IRON NECK! and a wall full of framed photographs, nearly all of them having to do with factory workers or labor strikes.

I sat on the edge of the bed and studied them. There was a group of somberly dressed men posing five deep in front of a wooden building strung with a banner that said LA-BELLE STRIKERS HEADQUARTERS, FORT STEUBEN NO. 65. One of the men held an elaborately lettered sign that said WE WILL STICK TILL H-LL FREEZES OVER. Another photograph showed a group of men and women standing near a doorway at the Pike-Haskell, the men wearing long canvas aprons with slits up the front and heat shields tied to their wrists. There were other pictures of workers inside factories, strikers' parades, and a heart-shaped portrait of a young woman, accompanied by the legend *In Memory of Ida Brayman, 17 Years Old, who was shot & killed by an Employer Feb. 5th 1913 during the great struggle of the Garment Workers of Rochester.*

I could have easily stayed the rest of the day, inspecting the collection. Sikora had a good eye for an interesting image, and he had selected pictures that were well composed and printed and at the same time reflected respect for people. They gave me a good feeling about Sikora, and suddenly I was glad that he had been Avery's friend.

I used the midget bathroom and headed back downstairs.

It was six o'clock, and my stomach was rumbling. I thought about asking Sikora out to dinner, maybe at the steak house up the road from the Arrowhead.

He was closing up shop. He shut the window in the kitchen and locked his cash register. "Libby," he said, "there's one other thing." He walked to the front window and turned the OPEN sign over so it said CLOSED.

"What?"

He turned back toward me, but reverted to his earlier self and refused to look me in the face.

"Nothing," he said. "Nothing important." He pulled a set of keys from his pocket. "You know, you probably ought to get back to the motel while you can still see your way."

I felt any friendliness that had grown between us suddenly evaporate. Was he afraid I was going to put the moves on him? Heck, I was too tired to do that, at least tonight. I hung my camera back around my neck and left.

I ate alone at the Mr. Bronco steak house, which looked like a cross between a high school cafeteria and Porter Wagoner's rec room. The hostess glumly directed me to the counter-service area. I'd be glum too, I thought, if somebody made me wear a gingham square-dancing dress to work. I bought a "Miss Kitty's Delite," which, to my sorrow, turned out to be a diet plate—a sirloin steak that looked like a charcoal briquette and a baked potato so small you could have used it for an earplug. I compensated by ordering a Hoss Cartwright–sized mug of beer.

To avoid thinking about Avery, I thought about Sikora for most of the meal. What was a guy like that doing dealing photographs out of a town as small and, let's face it, far gone as Darby? In Columbus, or Pittsburgh, or even in Akron, he'd do better. Wasn't he bored beyond belief? And if he was such good friends with Avery, why wasn't he at the funeral? And what accounted for the tension that sprang up between us from nowhere at the end of the afternoon?

This "just friends" line about Pam Bates bothered me too. I was pricked by a disturbing thought: What if Sikora and Bates really were two-timing Avery, and the discovery had sent Avery into a depression? That would account for how uncomfortable Sikora had been discussing Pam and Avery with me—not to mention the guilt he'd be feeling. Another disturbing thought kept me on edge for most of the meal: I felt unaccountably attracted to Sikora. Too many years with Hugh, I thought. I was probably suffering from some postrelationship rebound syndrome.

Back at the Arrowhead, I called Doug Pope and scheduled a meeting to discuss whatever there was to discuss about Avery's estate on Monday, then called the airline to confirm my flight to New York in the morning and reserve a return ticket Sunday night. I left a message at the desk to wake me up at five-thirty, turned on the TV, watched a little bit of what I think was an old "Barnaby Jones," and fell hard asleep.

7

Whoever was at the desk didn't bother with my wake-up call, but I woke up anyway at a quarter of six to the sound of a gang of trashmen heaving the contents of the Dumpster outside my window into the jaws of their mighty truck.

I felt under the sheets for the remote control that I'd fallen asleep with, and clicked through the alternatives: something called "Sermonette," featuring a minister who looked like Sonny Bono; a frenzied-looking aerobic exercise class; and Daffy Duck. I chose the last, then dropped one foot out of the bed and dragged my toes along the decaying shag carpet, hoping to make contact with my shoes, but had no such luck. I groped my way barefoot across the darkened room into the bathroom, which smelled like the Union Square subway station, notwithstanding all the strips of paper that had been plastered across the drinking glasses, towels, and toilet seat, reminding me that everything was sanitized for my protection.

The ice-cold water that shot from the shower head helped me focus my thoughts fast. One: I'd never stay at this place again; two: I'd better figure out what to do with that dog; three: I was furious with Dan Sikora. He was Avery's friend, and he was the only person I'd felt any kind of connection with since I'd come back to Darby. So why did he all but push me out the door the night before? How can you feel betrayed by someone you hardly know?

At six-thirty I called Pam Bates's clinic on the chance that somebody else was an early riser too. Over a chorus of yips and howls, a young male voice told me that he was there by himself, feeding the dogs, but that Pam would be back in half an hour. I scribbled the directions he gave me on the back of my airline ticket, cleared out the room, and threw my bag into the pickup.

The lady with the cookie-jar hairdo was on duty in the office again. This time she wasn't the least bit interested in me but sat there on her folding chair, eyes locked on "Good Morning America," stabbing at a shapeless mass of green acrylic yarn with a huge plastic crochet hook. I handed her my key, paid my bill, murmured something like goodbye and thank you very much, and filled Avery's travel mug with coffee from the gratis percolator.

Pam Bates's clinic was five miles out from the center of town on a strip of road that held a couple of farmhouses and a firecracker factory. The main structure was a small, tidy-looking brick building that must have been something else at one time—wasn't every building in Darby something else at one time?—maybe a beauty shop or mail-sorting facility. A square white wooden sign with crisp black lettering hung from a post by the front yard. P. BATES, it said, VETERINARIAN. I wondered briefly if Avery had made it for her. It was the kind of thing he liked to do; anything that required patience, measurement, and precision. To the back of the building I could see an old barn, newly painted white, with dog pens attached to it.

There was no one in the front room, but a parrot in a cage beside the reception desk screamed and flapped its wings when I walked in, setting my heart thumping. I craned my neck over the desk for a view into the examination rooms, and didn't see anyone there, either. Then I heard a woman's voice.

"Snoopy little thing, aren't you?"

I turned around. A tall, large-boned woman in blue jeans and a lab coat was standing in the doorway, holding an armful of branches with orange and yellow berries on them. She stepped into the room and behind the desk, then bent down to lift a vase from the cabinet. Although she appeared to be in her mid-thirties, her hair was gray, and she wore it in a braid that swung down her back nearly to her waist.

I understood that she had said all that she meant to say and was waiting for me to nudge the conversation into motion again. I waited for her to turn my way as she shoved the branches into the vase.

"I'm Libby Kincaid. Avery's sister. We talked on the phone."

She wiped the dried leaves and berries that had fallen from the branches off the desk with one hand into the other and shook them into the wastebasket.

"Of course I know who you are. You called this morning to say you were coming, didn't you? I moved Lucas out back yesterday, if you want to see him."

Despite her short manner, Pam Bates in person somehow didn't appear as sharp as she had seemed on the phone. It had something to do with her voice, which, when she took the edge off it, was throaty and sweet, and vaguely seductive. And there was something appealing about her bigness and the awkwardness that went with it—how it kept her just short of being a conventional beauty. For once, I was impressed with Avery's choice of a woman, and I was angry with him for treating her badly. For years he had been attracted to small blondes with traditional ideas—pretty, polite creatures with little to say. At first blush, anyway, Pam Bates seemed like a vastly more complicated proposition. Maybe Avery had matured enough to be attracted to her but not enough to try to understand her.

She took a ring of keys from a hook and motioned me to

follow her into the back area. There was what looked like a surgery room at one side, and a different kind of examination room next to it, with a row of shiny chrome cages on a shelf. Pam gestured toward the cages as we walked through.

"Do you want a rabbit? He's got a hernia, but we can fix that."

We walked out the back door and toward the barn. As we approached, the dogs went crazy with barking.

Pam opened the door to the first pen, and Lucas staggered onto his three legs, but didn't walk. He was a beautiful yellow dog with a wide nose and enormous brown eyes. Where his right front leg had been was now a gash tracked with thin black stitches.

He wagged his tail at Pam and licked her on the hand.

"He's healing beautifully, and I took the dressing off yesterday. Here, don't be afraid of him; he's as gentle as can be."

I reached out my hand and he licked it, and then I stroked him behind the ear. He responded by wagging his tail and nuzzling against my leg. Pam Bates walked down the row of pens, talking to the other dogs. Then she came back to Lucas and me.

"Well, are you going to take him? Or should I find someone else for him?"

I'd never be able to take care of him. A country dog in Manhattan? And a crippled one at that? Who would take him when I went out of town? Who would walk him when I had a late night out?

Lucas was leaning hard against me now, as though he'd known me forever.

But hadn't I been cutting down on the out-of-town work? Weren't those late nights out few and far between nowadays? And wasn't I more than a little lonely when I surfaced from my darkroom at three A.M. and didn't have Hugh to talk with anymore?

If I can't help Avery now, I thought, the least I can do is take care of his buddy.

Pam Bates stroked Lucas on the neck.

"I start surgery at eight," she said.

"I'm leaving for New York this morning," I said. "But I'll be back Monday. Can you keep him until then?"

"For ten dollars a day."

She locked the pen behind us and started up the walk to the clinic. I followed her in. There was coffee brewing in a white coffee machine on her desk, but she didn't offer me any.

"Look," I said, "I know that you and Avery broke up. He called me and told me afterwards. He was pretty upset. But I didn't know about Avery cheating on you until Dan Sikora told me."

She leaned against the sink, folded her arms across her chest, and looked at me.

"Sweetheart," she said, saturating both syllables of the word with contempt, "I'm not the kind of person who makes a habit of turning herself inside out for strangers, but I need to set you straight about one thing. I couldn't have cared less that Avery had a fling with some sex-starved high school secretary. What I cared about was that he lied to me about it. I've had three lifetimes and then some of people lying to me. My mother left me when I was a kid and said she'd come back, and she didn't. My foster parents said they were going to adopt me, and they didn't. My husband said he loved me, and then he broke my jaw. Do you see where I'm going? Do you see what I mean?"

Her cheeks were flaming, but she didn't cry.

"Avery knew how I felt about lies. He knew how much I needed to trust him."

I wanted to say something about Avery to her, but I didn't know what. That I was sorry he'd hurt her? I wanted to tell her that she was a magnificent person, that I knew the kind of determination it took to accomplish what she had on her own, but the look in her eyes warned me off.

"He made me crazy," she said. "And you're making me crazy too."

She turned to the sink and started to wash her hands. Then she filled a syringe and held it up to the light to read the measurement.

I gathered she meant I was supposed to leave.

I drove to the airport confused and cringing from my conversation with Pam Bates. Infidelity is not high on my list of forgivable sins. If Hugh had cheated on me I would have drop-kicked him out the tenth-story window. But Pam seemed to have moved out of the orbit of ordinary values; for her, trust was the only human obligation. And then Avery lied to her. I wanted to kill him myself.

But she hardly seemed a killer. I agreed completely with Dan Sikora on one point: Nobody who treated animals with the obvious love that Pam Bates showed could harm one out of loathing for its owner.

I couldn't get Lucas out of my mind. How could anyone have hurt him? It didn't seem like an act that Avery was capable of, even if he'd been completely unhinged by depression. And if he had felt desperate enough to want to kill Lucas, hadn't he gone about it all wrong? Wouldn't he have shot him in the head and made sure he was dead before he turned the gun on himself? Wouldn't he have shot him again if he'd realized he hadn't killed him with the first bullet?

I felt dizzy and sick by the time I boarded the plane. When we landed in Newark, all I could think of was making a beeline to Canal Street, pulling the shades, taking the phone off the hook, and lying in bed all day. The exhilaration that I usually felt on the cab ride into the city never surfaced at all. The weather had turned unseasonably hot for the end of October, the cab window wouldn't roll down, and I ached to get out of my turtleneck and into a shower.

Guilt got the better of me. I barely made it to a noon meeting at *Americans* with Octavia Hewlitt, the magazine's features editor. She was wiggling her fingers above her desktop fingernail-polish dryer and barking at someone over her speakerphone when I entered her office. Octavia, an extraordinarily attractive woman somewhere between fifty and eighty, had arrived at the magazine as a secretary when she was a mere wisp of a Wasp and pulled herself up to her current position by her T-straps, nabbing and discarding three, some said four, husbands along the way. The last one, who was as rich as God, stepped in front of a cab in the Village and left Octavia untold wealth, including fourteen rooms in the Dakota and a farm in Connecticut, where I understood Octavia spent the weekends throwing parties and hollering at her servants.

The photographer friend who had helped me get my first assignment at *Americans* once described Octavia as looking like a plush, beautifully kept house cat, and it was true. Her hair was silky and fine, she was overweight enough to look soft but not fat, and she moved in a way that was both graceful and deliberate.

As usual, even before she said hello, Octavia looked me over as though I were something she was thinking about re-upholstering. The first time she did it, sometime the winter before, I was afraid that she was going to ask me out on a date, but now I understood that it was just one of her power maneuvers. This time her eyes lingered briefly on my belt, which I'd bought in an airport somewhere. It was tooled vinyl and reversed from black on one side to brown on the other. It's gimmicky, but I try to pack in one bag.

"Olivia," she said, "how marvelous to see you. Aren't you dressed a little warmly for the weather?"

Through preternatural powers, Octavia had managed to foresee that it would be seventy-eight degrees on Halloween and was wearing a beige linen suit without any wrinkles in it. Like everything else she wore, it had epaulets and big gold buttons.

I tried to think of a clever comeback, but my brain, stupefied by the flight and parboiled by the heat, wouldn't respond. I ran the little anti-Octavia litany that I had developed during the last few months through my head. Don't fidget, don't apologize, and, above all, remember that she's best friends with Harriet Bemis, and you want a show at the Bemis-Snow Gallery more than anything in the world.

Suddenly Octavia seemed to remember something, rose from her chair, and hugged me so hard she nearly drove the back of my earrings into my neck.

"Olivia," she said, "you poor darling. I'm so terribly, terribly sorry about your brother."

I was astounded. Aside from the jabs Octavia occasionally made at me about my appearance, our dealings with each other were strictly business. She gave me the assignment, and I did the job.

She sat down next to me on the cream-colored love seat that faced her desk.

"Olivia, dear," she continued, "before we get to work, I want to tell you about something that I don't often discuss with anyone."

I had never seen Octavia so ill at ease. She was twisting a ring with a sapphire the size of a cough drop around and around on her finger, and her voice was shaking a little. I suddenly felt very embarrassed, as though I had walked in on her while her partial plate was out or something.

"Olivia," she said, "on Easter Sunday in 1957, my brother Bobby killed himself. It hurt us—my mother and my father and me—very much. We have never been able to understand why he did it. We all quite adored him. He was very handsome and very smart and very kind."

She stopped for a moment and looked straight at me.

"Olivia, the point is this: You can spend the rest of your life feeling guilty and disturbed, wondering what signals you missed and what you could have done and whose fault it really was and what he'd be like now if he had lived. It will be slightly suffocating—as though your mental self is always a little overdressed for the weather.

"Or," she said, stretching a hand out into the air in front of her, fingers splayed, examining her nails in the sunlight, "you can forget it ever happened. Erase it from your mind quickly and absolutely. You have a choice, you know. It's completely up to you."

Her voice wasn't shaking anymore at all. She had reverted in a snap to the old Octavia, witchy and composed. She looked at her watch and reached for the white loose-leaf binders where she kept her master schedule of forthcoming articles.

"Olivia, do you understand what I'm saying?"

I shrugged my shoulders. "I think so, Octavia." But I didn't, really.

"Good," she said. "Then let's get to work."

She had three jobs lined up for me, fortunately none of them in a rush. The most complicated—work on a feature about homeless children—would keep me close to home. I barely paid attention when she described the others—something about a custom-car show and something else about farm foreclosures.

I picked up some messages that had come in for me at the photo lab, looked at some color prints that they had processed and printed for me, and then dragged myself over to the Chock Full O'Nuts on Forty-second Street for a cream cheese sandwich and an orangeade. The man sitting on the stool next to mine had a *New York Post* opened to an article about some unidentified nut who'd spent the previous week heaving concrete blocks off a rooftop on West Forty-seventh Street but had only killed one person so far. I made a mental note to avoid the area, left a tip under my plate so no one would swipe it before the waitress got it, and finally rattled home on the steaming, stinking IRT.

I stepped off the elevator into the loft, and the heat hit me full in the face as though I'd just opened the door of the sauna at the Y. On the off chance that a psycho killer would be able to pry the cast-iron grates off one of our fifth-story windows and crawl inside, Claire always seals everything tight before she leaves in the morning. I always open everything back up as soon as I get inside. I cranked the front windows open, and the cacophony of the crowd on Canal Street rose like blackbirds from a pie.

I'd only been here the six months since Hugh and I split up, but for some reason it felt more like home to me than anywhere I'd been in a long, long time. The loft was in an old shirt factory and stretched from the front to the back of the building. The pressed-tin ceilings were a mile high, and the space was pierced by thin white iron columns with fluting at the top. The light coming through the front windows was lush and golden in the mornings. Sometimes I lay on my bed and framed countless imaginary photographs with my fingers, wallowing in the sun.

Claire had bought the place ten years before from a photographer, and there was a darkroom in the center. I rented from Claire and had the space to the front and the use of the darkroom. Claire had the space to the rear, and we shared the kitchen, which was really just a collection of pots and pans, a stove, a sink, and a refrigerator pulled together in a corner.

Neither Claire nor I had much in the way of furniture, but we had what made us feel comfortable. She had a wall of art books, many of them exhibit catalogs from the Metropolitan Museum of Art, where she worked as an assistant curator in the prints department; a desk; and some African sculptures, relics from her previous incarnation as a Peace Corps worker. I had a mountain of books on a million topics, from a biography of Elvis Presley written by his secretary to an outdated *Encyclopaedia Britannica* (Hugh had called my reading habits "promiscuous"), an army trunk full of clothes and a board I put on top of it to make a table, a mattress on the floor, and a collection of plastic snow-scene paperweights that I'd started as a joke to help me kill time in airport stores and that had somehow taken on a life of its own.

The few times that I'd ever felt flush, I'd put the money into my equipment, or vintage prints by documentary photographers from the thirties and forties; I kept the prints in a portfolio case leaning against the wall and reprimanded myself occasionally for not putting them in a safer place. The few other household things I'd acquired during my dozen years in Manhattan—a rug, a bookcase, a big metal sign shaped like a ham sandwich, and a couple of chairs—I'd left with Hugh. For some reason it seemed important at the time to slough off anything that reminded me that we'd ever lived together at all, but sometimes I missed the ham sandwich.

Claire had left a note under a bowl of apples on the drainboard next to the sink. *Lib*, it said, in purple felt-tip pen, *I'm at Sig's tonight but want to talk. Don't go anywhere for dinner tomorrow.* I felt a little lonely; I'd been expecting to spill my guts to Claire over a glass of wine. I stretched out on the only real piece of furniture in the place—a lumpy sofa covered in some sort of heavy, satiny, green-and-beige-striped fabric, which Claire's mother had cast off to us—and decided to nap until six or so, when I'd hit the darkroom.

I heard Octavia's voice as I was drifting off.

"You can feel guilty and disturbed, Olivia," she purred, "or not. It's up to you."

What disturbed me was that I had no idea which path Octavia had chosen. Is it really possible to consciously obliterate from your memory a devastating episode of your life?

I'll have her declawed, I thought, or get her a bell for around her neck, and I dropped into a dead sleep.

I woke up at eight to the sound of the telephone, which I ignored for fifteen rings until I was curious enough to find out who could be so persistent. It was Joey Dix, an old friend from R.I.T. who worked as a clerk in an art book store on Madison Avenue by day and fabricated neon sculptures at night. He had made it his business to keep tabs on me since Hugh and I split up. Nothing romantic—Joey gave up women a long time ago—but he has a gift for being a friend, which includes an eerie way of knowing when you're in trouble, even if he hasn't seen you in weeks.

Joey wanted to go out to dinner; I wanted to work in the darkroom. He wanted to meet at the Pink Teacup for breakfast tomorrow; I told him thanks a bunch, but I wasn't in the mood to be sociable.

"Lib," he said, "Claire told me about your brother. I know you're upset now, but you'll still need your friends when you get back up."

He was right, but I didn't want to inflict my current state of mind on anybody just now—especially not my friends.

I changed into a T-shirt and jeans, ate an apple and some Laughing Cow cheese cubes, unplugged the phone, and prepared for my night's work.

The first time I ever printed a photograph, under Uncle Garth's supervision, I felt a sense of wonder and repose that has never failed to repeat itself. For me, the only experience that rivals printing is good sex, but printing is better because the picture is still there when you wake up in the morning.

I closed the door and pressed a double-play Bob Marley tape into the cassette player. Then I wiped down the counters and lined up my chemicals, developing tank, church key, and film canisters next to the sink. You'd never guess it from looking in my refrigerator, but I'm obsessive about cleanliness and order in my darkroom.

I mixed the developer with water in the tank, adjusting the heat of the solution until the temperature measured sixty-eight degrees—no mother preparing infant formula could be more careful. I turned off the overhead light, pried the ends of the film rolls open with the church key, clipped the leader ends off, and threaded the film onto the developing tank coils. Then I dropped the four coils into the developing tank and closed the lid.

I've performed this ritual as often, maybe more often, than I've washed my face. No matter how tired I am, no matter how many deadlines I'm up against or how crummy the weather is, when I'm alone in the dark with my film and my tanks and my bottles, I feel touched by a kind of grace.

Then came my favorite part. I took the tank in both hands and tipped it gently back and forth for half a minute, then banged it on the counter to get the bubbles out—the way Mom used to bang the bubbles out of her angel food cake batter. I repeated the shaking process every minute for nine minutes. You can do this with the lights on, but I've gotten used to doing it in the dark.

I took the cap off, poured the developer out, poured water—again sixty-eight degrees—in, rinsed the film, and rinsed it again, then added the fixer and went through the shaking and resting process for another ten minutes. I poured the fixer out, rinsed fifteen times with water, added the hypoclear, rinsed fifteen more times, and added the Photo-Flo, which prevents water drops from adhering to the film and printing like big amoebas on the picture.

By this time you'd think I'd have fallen asleep, what with the darkness and the resting and the routine, but as usual, I was wide awake with anticipation of the new images. I extracted the first strip of film and held it briefly up to the light. These were the pictures I'd taken at the motel of the Arrowhead sign and more than a dozen of the Rollercade next door. The second roll contained the shots of Grandad's house and the broken windshield on the car in the yard. The third looked like more shots of downtown Darby—the boarded-up theater and the vintage Coke machine outside the gas station.

The last roll was a shock—there was a six-inch strip of black in the center of the strip, fading to gray, and only five or six intact images on either side of the obliterated part. I looked more closely—a few pictures of the fox in Sikora's shop, a couple of shots of the light that had filtered through the jar of marbles, and a sequence of the neon sign at the Arrowhead had survived, but whatever else was on the roll was gone.

I pinned the thing up. *Shit.* Mistakes do happen, but *damn,*

I thought I had some good stuff there. Those pictures of Si-kora's shop window with the ceramic hands in it, the shots from across the street—and didn't I do something with that shower curtain in front of the kitchen? What did I do? Drop the camera? Heck, no; I'd remember if I'd dropped the camera.

I lay on the sofa and flipped through the *Vanity Fairs* that Claire stacked fifteen deep on the floor. A fashion designer with big plastic buttons glued on his nipples; Claus von Bü-low in black leather; Donald Trump with his trap open . . . Darby never seemed so far away. Neither did Manhattan, for that matter. Neither here nor there, I thought. Don't know if I'm coming or going.

I made some contact prints. The shots of the Arrowhead sign were trash; so were the pictures of Grandad's, but I'd print them for memory's sake. The Rollercade looked promising, and the fox—maybe, just maybe, that was worth working with.

After ten or fifteen tries, the Rollercade looked stunning printed eleven by fourteen. But no matter what I did with the fox, he turned out flat.

I cleaned up the counters and fell into bed at three A.M., still in my clothes and reeking of darkroom chemicals.

By Saturday morning the heat had passed, and I woke up at ten, contented as could be, sunlight lying across my legs like a big old cat, the smell of the air sifting through the window screens, crisp and cool. A perfect morning, I thought. Home, in my own bed, on a Saturday—no appointments, no deadlines. I rolled to the other side of the mattress. No Hugh, even.

I laughed out loud. I dreamed I'd been smoking a ciga-rette, an occasionally recurring dream that I've had ever since I quit smoking, six years ago. Sitting in a lawn chair in somebody's backyard, smoking a real long cigarette—

Then the past week's events screeched into focus in my

mind's eye. It's funny how that works—how you can wake up not remembering for a few moments that your house burned down the day before, or that you found a lump on your breast, or that your brother just died. And then the bad news drops from some nowhere place in your brain to center screen, and you're back where you were last night, anxious and overwhelmed.

I had successfully ignored my answering machine the evening before, but now its blinking green light was driving me nuts. I hit the playback button and listened to the erratic medley of wrong numbers, questions about where was I anyway, Hugh accusing me of pretending not to be home, two excruciatingly long messages from Claire's mother about when Claire's brother's plane was arriving and who would pick him up and where they would go out to dinner, a call from Octavia Hewlitt's secretary, a succession of blank messages, and, after a very long pause, Uncle Garth's voice, in the faltering way of people who don't like leaving messages on answering machines:

"Lib? This is your uncle. We just got back and got the news. *[Pause.]* We're sorry, honey. *[Pause.]* Elaine says she's sorry, too. *[Pause.]* Elaine says let us know if we can help. *[Pause.]* It's Friday afternoon."

Thanks a lot, I thought. Yeah, right, you can help. Then, angry with myself: Give them a break. There's nothing they can do. There's nothing you can do. There's nothing anyone can do.

Another blank message, and then a voice that I couldn't place immediately:

"Uh, hello, Libby. I had a hard time getting your number. There was something I wanted to talk with you about, and then you left. Pam says you're coming back next week. I guess I wanted to make sure I got a chance to talk to you. Don't bother to call."

No name, but of course it was Dan Sikora. What was eating him now? Darn right I wouldn't bother to call.

I changed, yanked on my high-tops, dropped my camera

around my neck, and walked out to Canal Street, trying to erase Darby, Avery, Uncle Garth, and Sikora from my consciousness.

I bought a brownie and coffee at the luncheonette on the corner and scalded my fingers trying to tear a spout in the plastic lid. The sugar from the brownie and the caffeine hit my bloodstream at the same time, and I started to feel that jangle that I usually identify with too many cups of capuccino over the Sunday *Times*. Yogurt for lunch, I told myself. Yogurt and juice. Or maybe yogurt and a Coke.

I walked down Canal. Past the vendors with their metal folding tables piled to the sky with anything you could think of—baby dolls, radios, flashlights, knee-high panty hose, phony Rolex watches, battery-powered robots, coat hangers, fiber-optic lamps that play the theme from *Doctor Zhivago*, aluminum buckets, carrot scrapers, and shorty pajamas. Past the man standing in a doorway holding a burning tube of newspaper, past the man in pink hair curlers, past the woman carrying the little poodle with the little Mohawk haircut. Past the artists and the old Asian ladies and the teenagers in from Long Island with the sulky expressions and zebra-striped leggings. Past the Chinese grocers selling live turtles, past the pyramids of figs and persimmons, and past a stained and peeling sign for DANCING CHICKEN INSIDE ONLY 15¢.

In a different mood I'd be taking pictures of everything in sight. Instead, the images themselves seemed on the assault, buffeting me from every side.

I took the IND at Houston Street and emerged near Sheridan Square. No matter what I did to repress them, thoughts of Avery and Darby and Lucas splashed to the surface over and over, the way a beach ball does when you're a child and you try to hold it under water.

How depressed had Avery been when he called me? Was I really so insensitive that I couldn't pick up on desperation?

I stopped at the Three Lives bookstore and sorted through the photography section.

It was Lucas that was really getting to me. Murder-suicide with a dog. The more I thought about it, the more preposterous it seemed.

Avery decides he can't take it anymore. He gets his gun and takes it into the kitchen. Why the kitchen, anyway? One last ham-and-cheese sandwich? Lucas hears footsteps on the kitchen floor and trots in, looking for a handout. Avery shoots him. But why? He's afraid Lucas will try to talk him out of it? He doesn't think anyone will take care of Lucas the way he does? Ridiculous. Avery never went in for histrionics. He didn't even read novels.

So Avery shoots him. In the leg. According to the newspaper report, the cops said Lucas dragged himself across the floor to be by Avery's body. There was no point in that kitchen where Lucas could have been more than ten feet away from Avery. It would have been easy to shoot to kill. If Avery had felt strongly enough about Lucas to kill him, and wounded him with the first shot, wouldn't he have felt strongly enough to put him out of his misery? That was the part that gnawed at me hardest. I couldn't believe that Avery would leave Lucas, wounded and suffering, to bleed to death on the linoleum floor.

A clerk with short black hair and round brown glasses stepped my way. Was I looking for anything in particular?

I slid the book of Helen Levitt photographs that I'd been holding into its place on the shelf and stood up.

"No, thanks; I'm just thinking."

I pretended to look at the new arrivals.

Of course, there was Marianne Dallas's possibility. Somebody shot Avery, and Lucas too. Lucas tried to protect Avery, and whoever it was shot Lucas. It made sense, and it made no sense at all.

I bought a paperback picture book about dirigibles to justify my time in the store, and lingered briefly over a small book of hand-tinted photographs propped up next to the cash register, thinking that Dan Sikora would like it.

I remembered the way he'd turned his back on me at the door as I was leaving his shop.

Screw him, I thought, and headed back home.

Claire came in about six, bearing three grocery bags and full of nervous chatter about her week in Maine and her brother, Pip, who'd been in town last night, and about how they met up with her mother at Asti's, and how the red clam sauce was fabulous but they couldn't hear themselves think, let alone talk, over the singing waiters.

"Mother adored it, of course. She had squid sauce just to provoke us, and half a big old bottle of Chianti, so Pip went home with her in the cab instead of staying at Elena's, and Sig was so tired of us all he wanted to spit, and . . ."

She tore off her boots and ran over to me, tears streaming down her face.

"And I've been so worried about you I've been like this for days. Crying and carrying on."

The look on Claire's face and the bear hug she gave me were more than I could take. For five minutes we both sat there on our white metal folding chairs, sniffling and hiccuping. I finally took some deep breaths and regained control, more or less. Claire continued to sob.

Good old Claire. She once told me that if she didn't have a good cry once a day she was afraid her kidneys would back up. Sometimes in the evenings she put her record of André Watts playing Chopin on the stereo and started bawling as soon as the needle hit the groove.

"Oh, God, Libby, the descending sevenths! They're so . . . wrenchingly beautiful!"

I'm afraid I'm not doing Claire justice. Although her waterworks routine sometimes drives me up the wall, for the most part she is enormously loving, generous, and even-minded.

I'd met her through Hugh, at a picnic he threw at the Cloisters the spring after both of them had finished their graduate studies at Yale. Hugh had created a mesmerizing menu of appropriate French country fare: outrageously expensive cheeses, pâtés, olives, wines, and whatnot. Claire had shown up with a six-pack of chocolate Yoo-Hoo and one of those cakes that have the head and torso of a doll erupting from the center and the frosting decorated to look like a skirt. Hugh was ticked off; I was delighted.

Claire and I became fast friends immediately. By now she'd seen me through five apartment hunts, a ruptured appendix (Hugh kept telling me to sleep it off), and more ups and downs with Hugh than a trip on the Wonder Wheel at Coney Island. And when it was over between Hugh and me, she invited me to Canal Street.

"For as little or as long as you want, Libby. No strings attached. The place gives me the creeps when I'm alone here, anyway—like living in an abandoned Castro Convertible showroom."

Claire was starting to calm down. I poured two glasses of Blue Nun and plunked them down on the kitchen table, then placed the stuffed grape leaves that Claire had bought on a saucer and set that down too. Claire ate two and washed them down, then gave me a teary smile.

"You know me too well, Libby. Nothing like a little food to make me come to."

And Claire knew me too well to ask me for a blow-by-blow replay of my time in Darby. Still, she was comforting. Did I want to spend some time at her mother's house in Maine? Didn't I need a rest to help me accept the whole thing? Did I want her to help me find some sort of counselor?

I sat and watched and thought as she made two salads and some pasta, and roasted some garlic to spread on bread.

Slowly, over the course of the meal, I explained my discomfort over Avery's death. Not just the fact that he was dead and I would never see him again and there was too much left unsaid; during the past twenty years I'd had enough experience with loss to know that I would mourn and then the pain would recede and then I would bury the memory of Avery somewhere deep and dark, hoping it wouldn't surface except on a bright, sunny day when I was feeling good about myself.

I told her what Marianne had said about the fight that Pam and Avery had had. I told her about Dan Sikora and what he had said about Avery's plans to build a shop and his plans to go to the Outer Banks. I told her that he'd been in the middle of a project with Kevin Kogut, and that nothing that anybody in Darby had said to me could satisfy me that Avery was in any kind of condition that would cause him to kill himself. I reminded her of the phone call I'd gotten from him in August—how he'd seemed sad, but he hadn't seemed desperate. And I told her about Lucas, and how in a million years I could never believe that Avery would shoot him, let alone leave him suffering while he ended his own life.

Claire nodded and frowned and stirred her coffee.

"That's all the cops are going on?" she said. "That he broke up with his girlfriend?"

"That's all," I said.

I told her about Octavia Hewlitt's chilling assessment of my alternatives. Was I really free to choose to ignore the whole experience?

Claire rolled her eyes and shook her head.

"Lib, listen to me. Octavia Hewlitt is a she-devil, and you know it. You let her get under your skin, and you torture yourself by continuing to work for her when you and I both know that you could pick up the phone right now and get better work anywhere else.

"But that isn't even important. What's important is that you go back to Darby and dig and dig until you satisfy yourself. Maybe Avery killed himself and maybe he didn't. But if you think nobody knows anything now, just wait until five years from now, when you're so confused and pent up over the whole thing that you finally try to piece together what happened. Nobody will even remember that Avery existed, much less where anybody was on the night he died."

I was taken aback by the vehemence in her voice and the intensity of the expression on her face.

My heart was racing like a Harley-Davidson at a stoplight. Claire was right, of course. Why condemn myself to a life-time of unease and unanswered questions if I could find out what happened now?

Claire cleared the table, then said good night and walked off to her room.

I edged the police lock on the front door into place and turned out the lights. Through the front window I could see a party going on in the loft across the street. The faces had no features, and the sheer, billowing curtains distorted their figures. I stood in the center of the room and watched them for a long, long time.

8

It was dark by the time I flew into Pittsburgh on Sunday night. I bailed Avery's pickup out of long-term parking and, the novelty of the Arrowhead having worn off, drove straight to Garfield Road.

Avery's house had been swallowed by the night. Aside from the bushes and trash barrels at the end of the drive, outlined by my headlights, the only relief from the blackness was the small red dot of light that shone from Avery's front doorbell, like the point of a cigarette.

I turned off the headlights and sat in the truck for a while, allowing my eyes to adjust to the darkness. It's funny how it happens: how if you sit still and relax, the shapes and contours will rise from the emptiness, shift, darken, and arrange themselves into a familiar landscape before your eyes, in the same slow, evocative way that an image will surface on a piece of photographic paper as you hold it immersed in its developing bath.

I entered through the front door and, unwilling to disturb the tranquillity of the night by turning on the lights, felt my way through the shadows until I reached the kitchen. There, by the light of the open refrigerator, I helped myself to some crackers and cheese and began to wash the dishes that had been left in the sink—since when? The day Avery died?

The calendar attached to Avery's refrigerator had flopped closed. I smoothed it open and reattached it to the clip that held it to the door. Avery's small handwriting ran diagonally across the square that held tomorrow's date. "Pam's birthday," it said. I wondered what she would do to celebrate.

I was on the road to Doug Pope's office in Lisbon by eight in the morning. The bank was a narrow, red-brick building with tombstone-shaped windows and LISBON SAVINGS AND TRUST carved in a granite tablet above the second-story windows. It appeared to have been recently swallowed by a larger institution; a backlit red-and-white plastic sign that said *ServiBank* in dramatically slanting letters was bolted above the front door, and the display in the front window of incentives for opening accounts—food processors, televisions, digital clocks, and electric curling irons—made the place look like a Green Stamp showroom.

There'd been a branch of the Lisbon Savings and Trust in Darby once. When we were kids, Avery and I had Christmas Club accounts there, the kind where in December they give you your money back in brand-new bills in an envelope with a picture of Santa on the front. No doubt the Darby bank had been gone for years, along with the movie theater and the ice cream fountain.

I padded over an expanse of indoor-outdoor carpeting to an area of private offices at the far end and found an empty glassed-in cubicle with a wood-look sign on the desk: ATTY. DOUGLAS G. POPE. It was an austere arrangement: an in box, an out box, a golf club head that doubled as a paperweight, a plaque on the wall that said LISBON BOYS' CLUB AWARD OF MERIT, DOUGLAS G. POPE, ESQ., 1986, a calculator, and a small stack of unopened morning mail, including a *Golf Digest*, on the center of the desk. I was just trying to talk myself out of lifting up the photo-cube to inspect Pope's family, when he walked into the office.

Pope slid his eyeballs slowly from my head to my toes and

back, gave a little smile that was supposed to signify that he liked what he saw, and sat down in the chair next to mine. The hair rose on the nape of my neck, but I decided to grin and bear it, or at least bear it.

"You know," he said, "I lived in Darby when I was a kid. Your grandfather taught me history."

He smelled like breath mints and Aqua Velva.

"You were probably just a baby then. Just a little girl."

He lingered over the word "girl" as though it had breasts and buttocks.

"So I know all about your family," he said.

I studied the backs of my hands. "That's nice," I said. "I don't remember yours."

He lifted a file folder from his in box, leaned closer to me, and showed me Avery's will, a three-page document dated two years before.

"Avery called me up after I did a seminar on estate planning for the teachers' association. He said he hadn't realized that everything would go to his father if he didn't have a will, so he asked me to do one up."

It was a simple arrangement. He'd left me "all his property, real and personal," except for the fishing equipment, which he left to Kevin Kogut. He also left me "the residue" of his estate. I thought of the dirty dishes in the sink and suppressed a sick chuckle.

"Then there's the matter of life insurance," he said. "Your brother had one policy that he took out a year ago. It names your father as beneficiary. I don't suppose you'd know where he is, do you? I understand that he is, shall we say, a traveler."

The way he said it made clear to me that he knew exactly the nature of my father's "traveling," and why not? My father's behavior had been grist for countywide gossip for decades. In a place as small as Darby, what could be bigger news than a preacher's boy with a motorcycle who got the teacher's daughter pregnant when she was seventeen, served five years in the federal penitentiary for selling rare coins that were as common as dust, drank like a gutter, and drove her back to her father's house when she had two little children and nothing else?

I told him that I thought I could track him down.

"And he had another policy through the teachers' association that names you as beneficiary."

Pope leaned toward me ever so slightly, revealing a blood-clotted lump of styptic tape on his neck. Now he edged his knee toward mine, just enough so that the fabric of his trousers grazed my thigh.

"He's left you a nice little nest egg," he said. "Something a single girl like you doesn't get very often."

He was breathing through his mouth.

"What do you say we go out tonight and celebrate?"

He looked me straight in the eyes for an interminable amount of time—a technique I imagined he'd picked up from too many Clint Eastwood movies, or maybe too many nights watching Julio Iglesias on "The Tonight Show."

He was repulsive beyond description.

"Not on your life, Mr. Pope. What do you say we finish up my brother's business? I only have five minutes left on the meter."

Pope pushed out his lower lip like a little boy who didn't get the Matchbox car he wanted, shrugged slightly, and returned to the side of the desk where he belonged. He reached for the file folder and pulled out what looked like a photo-copy of something.

"You'll also be entitled to the money in his bank accounts," he said, barely skipping a beat. "What little there is. Less our fee, of course."

He read down the top sheet, then flipped to the second page.

"You'll notice that your brother wrote a rather large check on his account in March of this year. By 'large' I mean five thousand dollars—nearly the entire balance of his account.

"He wrote the check to Daniel Sikora, that long-haired guy who runs the junk shop on Central Street in Darby. As essentially the sole beneficiary under your brother's will, I'm sure you'll want to find out what the transaction was all about. It may have been a loan, in which case Sikora owes money to the estate, i.e."—he actually said "i.e."—"to you."

Pope looked up at me and curled one side of his mouth into a barely perceptible smirk.

"Daniel Sikora might be your kind of guy," he said. "Maybe the two of you can work something out."

The nerve of this bonehead! First he puts the moves on me, and then, when I don't respond, he tries to hurt me by making me out to be some kind of slut. I folded my copies of Avery's papers and put them in my bag.

He couldn't stop talking.

"And if you'd like," he said, "I'm sure we can enlist the services of a private investigator to help you find your father."

Barbara Stanwyck–style, I walked to the door, straightened my shoulders, and turned to Pope.

"Less your fee, of course, Mr. Pope? Thank you, but I'm certain that I'll be able to handle the rest of Avery's business without your help."

Damn it, I thought, as I walked back out to the truck, of course you'll have to deal with him again; there will be all kinds of forms to sign, for taxes and whatnot.

I climbed into the truck and sulked.

I filled the tank with gas at a self-serve pump and headed back the forty miles to Darby. Pope infuriated me, but I knew I'd get over it. Arrogant, self-righteous sleazebags are a dime a dozen. Someday he'd go too far with a customer's grieving widow and somebody would arrange to suspend his license. I hoped.

The five-thousand-dollar check bothered me a lot more. Then again, there could be a million explanations. I stumbled through an inventory of possibilities.

Sikora had a store; maybe Avery bought something from him.

Like fun he did. Avery's things—they were just Avery's things: posters, books, used furniture. He'd even bought his computer secondhand from the school. If there'd been any rare antique photographs worth five thousand dollars in Avery's apartment, you can be sure I would have noticed.

The truck. Maybe Avery bought the pickup from Sikora. I reached into the glove compartment and fished for the registration. No such luck. It showed Avery as having registered the truck almost two years before the check to Sikora.

Cocaine? Heroin? Who knows? Some of the straightest-looking people I've met—a nurse, a cop, a grandmother of four—were junkies. How could I pretend to know Avery well enough to say he didn't buy drugs? But to document a drug sale with a check? I did know Avery well enough to know he wasn't that dumb.

I pulled onto Central Street and saw the sun glance off Time Travel's front window.

The word "blackmail" drifted, dark and ugly, through my mind, and I realized that I was holding the steering wheel more tightly than I needed to. For blackmail to work, you need a secret—a very dangerous secret. Like you killed somebody or stole some money, or God knows what. The kind of secret that might drive you to suicide. The possibilities were limited only by the flexibility of the imagination.

I parked the truck by the curb and ground a dime into the meter. The distance between Avery and me had never seemed more unfathomable.

Sikora's shop was empty when I arrived. Tense, I occupied myself with a jar of marbles. I scooped out a handful and walked to the window.

Some were small, dull, mud-colored things, like malted-milk balls. Some were heavy and fat, shot through with spirals of color and tiny bubbles on the inside, pockmarked and scuffed on the outside. I lifted them to the light, one by one. One was clear glass, with a little rooster molded into the center; another had a miniature anchor inside.

I rehearsed my speech to Sikora.

"Sikora," I'd say, "level with me. Were you or weren't you bleeding money from my brother?" Or:

"Listen, Dan, you know extortion is a federal offense, don't you?"

I heard a sound like thunder on the back stairs, and Sikora filled the doorway like a bear, a huge grin on his face. He had a sandwich in one hand and a bag of Oreos in the other.

"Boy, am I glad to see you," he said. "Hold on a minute."

He ran upstairs to his apartment and came down again with a second sandwich and a can of Pepsi. He arranged the food on napkins on the counter by the cash register. I set the marble jar back on its shelf and pulled the piano stool up to the counter. Sikora was still smiling, but now he looked worried too.

"I got your message in New York," I said. "It sounded like there was something you needed to tell me."

He ate his sandwich. Then he slit open the Oreo bag with a letter opener and arranged a circle of cookies on one of the napkins, overlapping each other.

I tried not to drum my fingers on the counter. Had I become a typical New Yorker, so tense and hurried that I couldn't let someone gather his thoughts before he spoke? Or was Dan Sikora the slowest, most infuriating person I'd ever met?

He took a drink from what I thought was my Pepsi, and finally spoke.

"You probably don't know it yet," he said, "but if you go through Avery's papers you'll find out. Avery loaned me some money last spring. And if you're wanting to know why I didn't tell you before, it's because last week I was feeling so low about Avery and so guilty about whether I could have done something to help him that I couldn't bring it up. You know how it is; the longer I didn't say something, the harder it was to mention it at all."

He spoke in low, measured tones, hardly pausing for breath.

"There, I've said it," he said.

I felt the tension begin to drain from my shoulders, but still, something kept me wary.

"It was a deal," he said, "and I needed some cash. A guy I know, Bart Glass, called me up and said he'd come across some Adam Clark Vroman photographs at an old guy's up in Youngstown. You know Vroman, don't you?"

Of course I did. As far as printing went, I idolized him. His turn-of-the-century portraits of Hopi Indians were lustrous, sensuous, and immaculately composed. I had a book of reproductions that I turned to over and over for the pleasure of it.

"Glass didn't have the cash, so he wanted to cut me in. I went up with him to this man's house. A huge old place—as big as a sanatorium or something. Only decrepit. Half the glass gone from the greenhouse, pans underneath the radiators, flypaper hanging from the chandeliers, and wallpaper dropping off the walls from the leaks in the roof. Old steel money gone to rust, I guess.

"He kept the photographs in a box under his bed. He said they'd been 'Father's.' He said that Father had lived in San Francisco 'some time ago' and that Father had been 'especially fond' of these. He laid a blanket out on the bed, and he laid the pictures on the blanket."

Somebody came in the front door of the shop, poked through a box of postcards, and left.

Sikora continued:

"They were beautiful. I can't tell you how beautiful. Beautiful images; beautiful prints; beautiful condition. But that wasn't all. The real treasure was in the bottom of the box. Two glass negatives of images that, as far as we could tell, hadn't come to light before. The kind of thing that happens to a dealer once in a lifetime, if he's lucky.

"The old guy knew he had something good, but he didn't

know how good, and he needed some money fast. He wanted fifteen thousand dollars for the set. A steal, considering you could turn the whole thing over immediately for twice that, easy, if you knew where to go with it, and I did. Glass needed someone to kick in eight thousand dollars, and he tried me. I could come up with three, but no way could I come up with more unless I white-saled everything I owned.

"So I thought of Avery. I thought, Here's the perfect investment for Avery Kincaid. He's interested in American Indians; he likes good photographs; and who doesn't like making some pain-free money fast?

"Avery jumped on it. I didn't find out until later, but it was back when he and Pam were still seeing each other, and, like I told you before, they were thinking about settling down and buying a place with a lot of land so they could have the clinic and the house all in one place. What he'd make on this deal would go a long way toward helping out with the down payment.

"The deal with Glass was simple: We'd buy the pictures; I'd put him in touch with a guy in Philadelphia who I knew would pay a premium to get his hands on the new Vromans; Glass, Avery, and I would each pick one print to hold on to for the long term; and bang—we'd double, maybe triple, our investment in six weeks' time and still have more to come."

Sikora stopped talking and ran his fingers through his hair.

"That was March," I said. "What happened?"

"It seems like I made a mistake," he said. "Glass wouldn't stick to the deal. The dealer in Philadelphia offered him forty grand, and he wouldn't take it. Glass called me and he said he wanted to hold out longer—maybe a year or two.

"I forgot to tell you, Glass is pretty much of a jerk. He has a simpleminded theory of investing. If someone offers you so much now, they're bound to up the offer a year from now."

"That's ridiculous," I said. "He can't just sit on them forever, calling all the shots. You had a deal, didn't you? He said he'd sell right away. Can't you hold him to his agreement? Can't you threaten to sue him or something?"

"I don't think so, Libby," he said. "We didn't have anything in writing, anyway. Besides, who's to say he won't make a better deal in the end? But meantime—"

"But meantime," I broke in, "he's got your cash, and Avery's contribution, tied up but good. Which is fine, if you don't need it for anything, I suppose. And as long as you can still trust him to sell the pictures in the end and cut you in the way he said he would."

Sikora didn't comment.

I continued:

"So what did Avery have to say about Glass's big idea?"

Sikora looked down at the floor for a while, then back at me. I could tell he was making an effort to be candid with me after his evasive performance the previous week. It was hard on him. I think by nature he was one of those guys who, when the going got tough, clammed up.

"He was pissed, of course. At first, anyway. Who wouldn't be? That was when he told me about his plans for the money—about the place for Pam. God, I felt like a heel.

"And then the next day he called me up and said let's go out for a beer. So we went out for a beer and shot some pool over at the place we used to go to up in Salem before he started seeing Pam so much. He didn't mention the pictures all evening. And then, when we were leaving the bar, he turned to me, and he was laughing, and he said, 'Dan, cut the hangdog crap. I trust you. I know you'll get the money back.'

"He never mentioned it to me again. And he still came around to the store on Saturdays, trying to talk me into learning to fish, or checking the place out to see what I'd come up with in the way of pictures that week. When he broke up with Pam, I felt real guilty about it. I thought maybe she knew about the money and was mad at Avery for doing something dumb with it. But he told me no, it didn't have anything to do with it. And then Pam told me about Avery fooling around behind her back."

Sikora reached over and rang something into his cash register so that the drawer opened up, pulled out an envelope, and gave it to me. It had ten one-hundred-dollar bills inside.

"What's this for?"

"I'm paying back Avery," he said. "A little bit at a time. And when Glass finally does decide to unload those pictures, you'll get your pick of the prints and the rest of Avery's cut. Fair enough?"

For the first time, I noticed that the panorama photograph that had hung on the wall behind the counter the week before was gone. I wondered what he had hawked from his collection upstairs.

"Fair enough," I said.

A couple with a baby in a backpack walked in the door. I folded the envelope and tucked it into my camera bag.

I bought some groceries at the 7-Eleven and drove to Pam Bates's clinic. Her assistant was in the parking lot, hosing down the parrot cage with the bird inside. The parrot was whirling around and screaming in the spray like a motorboat propeller on the loose.

"You can get Lucas from Pam," she hollered. "He's looking pretty good."

I walked in the front door of the clinic and rang the bell at the desk. No one came.

I looked into the back rooms. There was a dachshund with a splint on his hind leg, snoring gently in a cage, but no one else.

I walked out the back door to the kennel. Pam emerged at the same time from the barn, with Lucas beside her, walking gingerly on his three legs. She was wearing blue jeans and a white T-shirt with a dalmatian silk-screened on it, and her gray hair, not in a braid this time, hung to her waist. She said nothing until she was ten feet away from me.

"He's doing pretty good," she said. "He went clear around the barn with me."

Lucas wagged his tail and walked over to me.

"He may be a little sore from not having moved much in the past week," she said, "but he shouldn't be in pain anymore from the wound."

He leaned his head against my calf and looked up.

"What do I do for him?" I asked. "I mean, does he need any special diet or anything? Any pills?"

Her lip curled slightly, as though she were about to say something rude, but then she stopped herself.

"Just the usual dry dog food," she said. "Nothing fancy. But go easy on him. It's going to take him a while to get used to his new gait."

She bent over and stroked the area around the wound with her index finger.

"See," she said, "it's all healed up."

The stitches were gone, and the fur was beginning to grow back where Pam had shaved it off. It didn't look as bad as it had the week before, but it still made me squirm.

"Your bill's at the front desk," she said.

Then she walked back into the barn.

I paid the bill, then pushed Lucas into the pickup's passenger seat by his back legs. He was happy to be there, sniffing around the upholstery and whining expectantly. He wanted Avery, I knew.

"Sorry, sweet guy," I said. "His sister is going to have to do."

I drove back slowly to Avery's, afraid of hurting Lucas or of knocking him off balance. He grew attentive as I turned up Garfield Road; by the time I turned into Avery's driveway he was in a frenzy of happiness. I could hear the telephone ringing while I parked the truck and helped Lucas out of the seat and into the house. It kept up while I unloaded the grocery bag from the back seat and fiddled with my keys until I found the one that fit the front door lock.

I picked up the receiver and heard a gasp, then the sound of a woman's voice on the line.

"Where were you?" she said. The voice was taut and wavered. I didn't recognize the owner.

"Hello?" I said. "Who's calling?"

"Libby," she said, "this is Marianne Dallas. I've been trying to get you for two days. The motel said you'd left, and finally someone said to call the lawyer, and then finally he said that you were back. . . ."

She was drifting off, her words slurring—with what? Alcohol, drugs, fatigue?

"Marianne," I barked. "Marianne, tell me what you want. Tell me what the problem is."

I heard a bang—the sound a telephone receiver makes when you drop it on something hard—and an exchange of words between Marianne and what sounded like another woman. Then a new voice, the voice of an older woman with a smoker's throat, came on the line.

"Hello, dear," she said. "This is Marianne's mother, Peg. Marianne wants me to tell you that Kevin's run away from home and she wants to talk with you about helping us find him."

And then, "Marianne, ain't that right?"

Marianne didn't seem to be holding up her end of the conversation. Marianne's mother came back on the line.

"Well, dear," she said, "why don't you come on over and talk with us here? Marianne isn't feeling well enough to come to the phone."

I thought about bringing Lucas with me to Marianne's, decided not to subject him to a second truck ride, and settled him onto his dog bed. Then I threw the groceries into the refrigerator and drove over to Thurman Road.

By broad daylight the Dallases' house looked even bleaker than it had the night of Avery's funeral. Two enormous green garbage cans lay on their sides at the end of the driveway, and the autumn leaves lay thick and matted across the cement front walk. As I approached the front door, I noticed that the metal street numbers bolted to it had rusted, staining it with long brownish streaks.

A short, stocky woman wearing a shapeless button-front cotton housedress with jungle animals printed on it—the kind of thing you see advertised in *Parade* magazine as a "Model's Coat"—and scuffed white patent-leather slippers opened the door. Her hair bore no trace of its natural color but had gone the dingy beige that hair goes after decades of bleaching and tinting and ratting. She had organized it into a modified beehive supported by a high-security arrangement of gold-tone bobby pins.

There could be no question that the woman was Marianne's mother. Her face sagged with age and smoking and too many summers in the sun, but I could tell that at one time she was a dead ringer for Marianne—from the big brown eyes to the slightly snub nose to the dimpled chin.

She passed an extra-long, extra-thin cigarette nervously from one hand to the other and gestured toward the front window.

"We were watching for you to come up the road," she said. "Marianne and me."

Marianne was nowhere in sight.

Peg walked into the kitchen, and I followed. What had looked like sociable disarray at last week's gathering for Avery's friends had disintegrated into an eddy of litter and crumbs. The sink was crammed with dishes and pans; no one had attended to the spaghetti sauce that had overflowed its pot on the stove and spilled down the oven door. The Mr. Coffee machine had been ignored for too long, and the pot was opaque with burned-on coffee. A pile of dish towels lay on the floor in front of the dishwasher, where someone had made a halfhearted attempt to mop up a puddle of something, and there were hundreds of Cheerios in various stages of decomposition spread over the table and heaped on the floor around the baby's booster seat.

I lifted a soggy box of groceries from one of the dinette chairs, placed it on the floor, and sat down.

Marianne's mother sat on a stool at the kitchen counter and ground her cigarette into an upturned ice cream carton lid. Through the chips in her red fingernail polish I could see a coral-colored layer underneath.

"It was like this when I got here," she said. "Marianne called me last night and told me to come over. Kevin still wasn't home and she said she couldn't take it no more and she wanted me to come help watch Teddy junior."

Marianne appeared at the kitchen doorway. She was wearing a lumpy-looking terry-cloth bathrobe, and she was barefoot. Her face was splotchy and there were crescent-shaped mascara stains beneath her eyes.

"Teddy's still sleeping," she said. Then she sat down and started to cry.

She cried for a full five minutes. Big, gasping sobs. I tore paper towels off a roll and fed them to her, one by one. After a while the sobs changed to hiccups, and then to an occasional sniffle and a shudder.

Her mother filled a glass with water and placed it next to Marianne's elbow. Then she shook some pills out of a bottle and put them next to the glass. Marianne reached out for the pills, and I placed my hand gently on top of hers.

"Marianne," I said. "What's going on? What's wrong?"

She started to cry again, and then she stopped.

"Kevin," she said. "He went off on his bike Saturday night and he never came home. I thought he was with Ted, at a game or something, and they forgot to tell me. So I went to bed. But Ted was at his night job and he didn't get in until three and by then Kevin was gone for hours."

She dipped a paper towel into her water glass and pressed it against her forehead.

"Ted thinks—the police think—they all think that he ran away to his father's in Detroit. Kevin hasn't been getting along with Ted, and sometimes he thinks that his father would treat him better. But he's not there, and nobody can check all the bus stations—the police wouldn't even start until today.

"He's so little," she said, "and I'm so scared for him."

Peg turned to me. "I told her we could see about getting some of those pictures printed up on milk cartons."

Marianne buried her head in her hands.

"Mother, please, I can't stand it."

All three of us sat without speaking for a while. Then Marianne took a deep breath.

"Libby," she said, "I called the principal of Kevin's school to find out if he knew anything—knew if Kevin had gotten in trouble or something. And he said that all he knew was that someone said they saw Kevin talking with you in Avery's office while you cleaned out his things. And I thought . . . well, I thought that maybe Kevin said something to you, about where he was going or if something was wrong, or—I don't know. Think, please think. Did he say anything to you?"

I thought back to my encounter with Kevin at the high school. I hardly wanted to tell Marianne how troubled Kevin had seemed to me—about Avery and about life in general. I remember how slight he had seemed, and how at a loss I was for words that could console him.

"Marianne," I said, "I talked with Kevin for a while, and he didn't say anything to me about going anywhere. He did mention that he had problems with Ted, and he did seem very hurt about Avery."

I suddenly felt hopelessly sick with myself. A child that sad, that lost-seeming—shouldn't I have helped him somehow? Called his mother, taken him to a doctor? Said the right things?

I remember what Scannell had said about having brought a minister to the school to talk about Avery's death, and shivered. It wasn't possible, was it? A child as young as Kevin couldn't be torn so deeply by grief that he'd take his own life, could he?

I felt as though a hand had reached inside my head and was pressing with all its strength against my forehead.

A child's cry came down the stairs.

"That's Teddy junior," said Peg. "He'll be wanting his snack." And she left the room.

Marianne held her hand out in front of her face. We could both see it tremble.

"Ted's in Lisbon," she said, "talking with the police."

I drove back to Avery's, gruesome thoughts about Kevin Kogut swimming through my head. Thank God it's Indian summer, I thought. If he's lost out in the woods somewhere, at least he won't freeze. As long as he's not hurt, as long as he wasn't stupid enough to take a ride with anybody—and who'd pick up a kid with a bike?

What a morbid mind I've got! The story of my life. The comment on my third-grade report card from Mrs. Penny, or Nickel, or whatever her name was: "Libby would do much better if she didn't think so much."

Relax, I thought. Ted's right. The cops are right. He's probably on a bus right now, headed for his father's. The boy had every incentive to run away from home—the classic demanding-stepfather syndrome; a wasted, listless mother; the death of Avery, his idol, his best friend.

Damn it, Avery, I thought. How could you do this to a kid?

So he hid his bike in a ditch somewhere and got a ride to a Trailways station. Right. His dad will be calling any minute from Detroit. Kevin will be sitting there at the kitchen table. He'll be tired, maybe he'll have a cold or something—but he'll be okay.

There was a yellow jeep parked in Avery's driveway. The front door to the house was open, and Lucas was sitting in the front yard. I felt a surge of panic. Then Pam Bates stepped out of the house carrying what looked like a heavy cardboard box. She acknowledged that I was there with a frown, jerked her head to get the hair out of her face, put the box in the back of the jeep, and returned to the house. I got out of the truck and leaned against the door. Pam came out with another box and shoved it into the jeep too. I walked over to her.

"Pam," I said, trying to keep my voice steady and friendly. "What are you doing?"

"What am *I* doing?" she said. "What are *you* doing? How long has this dog been shut in the house without any water?"

I looked at my watch.

"One hour and forty-eight minutes," I said. It was an interesting tactic—going on the offensive while she was clearly the one who needed to do the explaining. "What are you doing in Avery's house?"

"If you'd been here, I would have given you the chance to open the door," she said. "But you weren't."

She went back into the house, then reappeared carrying a frame backpack and an armful of record albums. The one on top was the Rolling Stones' *Exile on Main Street*. She threw the backpack into the rear of the jeep, then stacked the records on the front passenger seat.

"I'm only taking what's mine," she said. "The son of a bitch never returned anything."

She hoisted herself into the driver's seat, slammed the door, and gunned the motor. Lucas ambled over and whimpered at the edge of the lawn. Pam got out of the jeep, scratched him under the chin, and said something to him.

"Pam," I said, "it's okay. It really is. Of course you should have what's yours."

She got into the jeep again and backed down the driveway, never once looking my way.

Happy birthday, I thought. You really know how to have a good time.

I shepherded Lucas back into the house and refilled the water bowl that Pam had set next to his bed. She was right, I thought. I'd have to be more careful with him. I'd have to make sure he was fed and bathed and that his shots were up to date. I'd have to take him for walks. Where? The roof of my building? The West Side Highway? Good God, I'd have to buy a pooper-scooper.

Poor guy. He was hobbling around the house, sniffing and whimpering—still looking for Avery, I was certain.

The living room was warm from the afternoon sun; the fish tank babbled pleasantly in the corner. Nice, I thought. Pretty too. I ought to get one of those for New York. Maybe I'd put in one of those little plastic divers that blow bubbles out of their helmets.

Then I remembered. This fish tank was mine—or would be, as soon as that character Pope finished doing whatever he needed to do. I could ship it to New York if I wanted.

I sat down on the sofa and surveyed the room. How peculiar. All of Avery's things—the fish tank, the pictures on the walls, the jacket hanging on the hook in the hall—they belonged to me now. And I was the one who just six months before decided that possessions had no meaning and abandoned a decade of belongings to Hugh.

What would I do with this stuff? Sort it into boxes and put it in storage? Have a yard sale on Canal Street? Give the clothes to the homeless in Grand Central?

A small piece of white paper on the fireplace mantel caught my eye. The paper had PAM BATES, V.M.D. printed at the top and a little picture of a dog's head in the corner. A key was taped to the center.

I glanced around the room again, then looked in Avery's bedroom and the kitchen. I hadn't the vaguest idea what was gone. She hadn't taken anything big, anyway, like the bed. But then again, what did I care? What was hers was hers.

I decided to explore the basement. The previous week I'd been too distracted by the feeling of Avery in the house, too scared by the emptiness, to venture down the stairs.

There was no railing and the stairs were steep, so I descended slowly, gripping the wall on the right with my fingers. The day was darkening fast, but enough light glimmered through the narrow windows at the top of the basement walls to let me find the light pull that hung over Avery's workbench.

It wasn't a very sophisticated setup—just some big planks over a pair of sawhorses, a pegboard, and metal-bracket shelving on the walls—but it looked like an organized, useful place. Three fishing rods rested horizontally on hooks hanging from the pegboard—one blue, one green, and one natural wood, its handle intricately bound with colored threads. Below them hung a variety of reels, some small and streamlined, a couple big and clumsy-looking. The rest of the pegboard was covered with tackle—a feathery, gaudy, fierce-looking display of it.

I lifted a lure from the wall and laid it against the palm of my hand. It felt heavy and light at the same time—like a piece of jewelry. A hook that was really an exquisite cluster of smaller hooks dangled from a tiny clasp hidden in the feathers.

I held it for a long time. It had been easily twenty-five years since I'd handled a piece of fishing equipment. Avery and Grandad had developed a real connection through all this tackle—all these threads and beads and prongs. I had enjoyed being on the water in the boat with them, wearing the huge orange life jacket, holding a bamboo pole, but I had never wanted to spend hours threading the reels and assembling the lures the way Avery and Grandad did. It was nice for them, I thought: nice for Grandad to be able to share his obsession with someone, nice for Avery to learn something he could lose himself in for the rest of his life.

His life.

As I stood there turning the lure in my hand, a feeling of sadness more extreme than any sadness I'd ever felt before crept over me from the feet up, the way coldness overcomes you when you stand fishing in a stream for too long—so slowly that you barely know it's there, but so strongly that when you try to move your feet feel frozen to the ground.

*   *   *

Sometime later—I don't know how long—I heard the scrape of tires on gravel, and the headlights of a car swept past the basement window, startling me so that I let out a yell. I trudged up the basement stairs, perturbed at the intrusion.

Someone was banging at the front door; Lucas stood in the hallway, howling. I saw the door open, and there stood Sikora, carrying a cardboard box crammed with white Chinese take-out cartons and two bottles of wine.

He set the box on the floor and took off his boots.

"What is this, Libby, a séance? When I didn't see any lights on, I was worried you'd gone to bed without any supper."

He flicked on the living room lights and stood there, in his stocking feet, beaming, rubbing Lucas's head with his hands.

The lights hurt my eyes for a moment, and I realized that I had been crying and that my face was still wet.

Sikora took my hand and led me to the sofa.

"Hey there," he said. "You're not doing so good, are you?"

He held my hand and started to pat it, the way somebody's grandmother would. With that, I started to weep uncontrollably. That's all it usually takes to get me going when I'm feeling bad; somebody's nice to me and then I'm a goner.

"Me," I gasped, "and Marianne Dallas."

"What's wrong with Marianne Dallas?"

Between snorts and shudders and sniffles, I bleated out the story of my afternoon with Marianne Dallas and told him about Kevin being gone and the talk I'd had with Kevin about Avery and about how worried and guilty I felt.

"Goodness, goodness," he said, still patting the back of my hand. "My, my, my."

I wiped my nose with a take-out napkin.

"And then," he said, "you came back here to this big empty house full of Avery's things and you started to feel really bad."

"It's not that big," I said.

"Okay," he said.

Then he took the hand that he'd been patting, folded it across the other one in my lap, and stood up.

"I know what," he said. "Why don't you sit here and cry for a while longer, and I'll fix up the food. Honest. You can do it as long as you want. And then we'll eat. Pork Lo Mein. General Gau's Chicken. Delight of Three. From the Ding Ho. You'll like it. I know you will."

He looked so serious, and his voice sounded so concerned, that I burst out laughing.

He looked at me in disbelief.

"You remind me of my roommate, Claire," I said. "Giving me permission to cry. And all this food!"

I pointed at the box. There were some lumpy-looking things wrapped in aluminum foil and at least seven large white cartons.

Sikora was already rummaging through the kitchen for plates and things.

"Sounds like somebody I ought to meet," he said. And then, "Hey! What happened to the knives and forks?"

I opened the silverware drawer. The whole tray of utensils was gone. I opened the drawer next to it; they weren't in there, either.

I opened the cupboards over the sink; they were empty except for some gas-station-premium drinking glasses that said PITTSBURGH STEELERS on them and a half-empty box of scouring pads.

For a moment I was dumbfounded. Who would take the dishes and leave the portable television? Pam, of course. Those boxes she packed must have been mighty full. I told Sikora about the episode in the driveway. He rolled his eyes, then turned sober.

"Poor Pam," he said. "I figure she didn't come get the stuff a long time ago because she was hoping she and Avery would get back together."

I remembered all the things I left with Hugh when we split up. I couldn't imagine being in the same room with him again, let alone moving back in.

"Not likely," I said. But maybe for Pam it was true.

Dan walked out the front door to his car. When he returned, he had a huge pocket knife in his hand, the kind with spoons and forks and dental drills on it.

"I'm not outsmarted that easily," he said.

He dug into the side of the knife, pulled out a corkscrew, and went to work on the wine bottle. Then he started to clear the books and things from the coffee table to make room for dinner. One of the books was thick and old-looking and had a dark-red binding. Sikora opened the cover and coughed at the dust, then read out loud:

" 'The Gaithers Coal Company: Its Founders and Their Legacy. The Marshall County Historical Society Library.' "

He pulled a slip of paper from an envelope at the back of the book.

"This thing's been overdue two weeks," he said. "Do you want me to take it back?"

"What is it?"

He handed it to me. Little bits of paper flaked off the edge of the first page as I turned it.

"Avery was doing some kind of research into old coal mines. I don't know why. He asked me a little while ago if I knew where he could get his hands on some maps that would show where the mines used to be. I told him to ask at the Historical Society, and it looks like he did. Do you want me to bring it back?"

"Is it something to look at?"

"What?"

"The Historical Society."

Sikora bit his lip and thought for a moment. "It's got Pretty Boy Floyd's death mask—if you like that kind of thing. And a piece of bread from the Civil War. Not to mention a lot of pictures made out of human hair."

"Sounds good to me," I said. A quick tour of the Marshall County Historical Society tomorrow might be just the thing to revive my spirits.

Sikora put the book on the mantel and opened the wine; I sat on the floor next to the coffee table, extracted the chopsticks from their paper sleeves, and plunged into the first carton.

I ate everything in sight. General Gau's Chicken, Pork Lo Mein, Peking Raviolis, Moo Shi Shrimp, boiled rice, fried rice—the works. I ate like the survivor of a hunger strike, like a woman who's been lost in the woods for three days with only the berries and grass to eat.

Sikora found some wineglasses that Pam had overlooked in her raid—or maybe they'd been Avery's. The house cooled off in the dark, and I dragged some wood up from the basement and built a fire in the fireplace.

We ate, and we drank wine, and we talked. Talked about the merits of Hunan- versus Szechuan-style beef, boiled versus steamed raviolis, and whether it's better to fold in the ends of your Moo Shi pancakes before you roll them or after you roll them.

Lucas begged for scraps, which we gave him, and retired to the kitchen to sleep on the rug in front of the radiator.

We pulled the fortunes from our cookies and laughed at the messages: "You would make a good dentist" for me; "Your income will increase" for him. We agreed that maraschino cherries in the sweet and sour sauce were an abomination, and dropped them into the fire.

We talked about Raymond Chandler, Ken Kesey, Hank Williams, Jr., and Shelley Duvall. We talked about championship wrestling, colorized movies, and the return of the Cadillac fin. We talked about Walker Evans, and we talked about Zippy the Pinhead. Our conversation was a mile-long mixed metaphor—an endless string of non sequiturs and comforting nonsense.

Sikora poured some more wine while I stirred up the fire, and then we moved onto the couch. We sat silently for a while, relaxing. Something about looking at the fire in the fireplace reminded him of Shawnee, Sikora said—a speck of a town in south-central Ohio that got so rich so quick on coal that it raised an opera house on a rumor that Jenny Lind might drift west the next year. A place where the coal was so thick that people mined through trapdoors in their cellars, and where, in the 1880s, the miners, made desperate by their meager lives, heaved oil-drenched coal cars down to the pit, where the coal burned underground for the next sixty years, smothering the town in a cloud of smoke and haze. Sikora had some old photographs of Shawnee miners, he said, and a hand-colored one of the town, taken at a distance not long after the fires were set. It looked like Pompeii, he said, or Hanoi.

He told the story, and we sat close to each other, wrapped in Avery's blankets, watching the flames in the fireplace nuzzling the surface of the dead-black logs, watching the circles of blue light coil themselves around the wood like bracelets on a black woman's arms, watching the intermittent explosions of sparks fan out against the back of the fireplace, fade, fan out, and fade again.

And then we stopped talking altogether, and lay there against each other, feeling each other breathe, stroking each other's hair, saying nothing, just listening to the soft hiss and snap of the logs, our bodies warmed by the pulsing orange heat of the fire and by our longing to hold and to be held and to unfold ourselves into each other. I emerged from the blankets only long enough to drop my sweater on the floor; Sikora pulled me back beneath him, and we made love for hours, witnessed only by the unblinking eyes of the skeleton fish.

9

The first frost had hit overnight, wringing the landscape of the gleam of Indian summer. The leaves of the rhododendrons at the end of the driveway shrank and hung close to the stems of the plants, the leaves that were left on the oaks in Avery's backyard turned from amber to a dull, dead brown, and the lawn was ashen with ice. Sikora spent half an hour trying to get his van going before he left.

I cleaned up the small breakfast mess that he and I had made, turned up the thermostat, and tried not to think about where Kevin Kogut had spent the night.

Avery's house didn't seem as unsettling to me now as it had the week before. The fact that Avery was dead no longer seemed so unreal. Now that I had disturbed the still lives that he had left behind—the unmade bed, the lidless can of shaving cream on the bathroom sink, the open magazine on the couch—his presence, or, that is, his absence, didn't seem so obvious.

I drifted around the living room for a while, feeding the fish and drinking coffee, and then I rummaged through Avery's bureau for something warm to wear. I found an L. L. Bean navy-blue-and-white pullover with a moth hole at the shoulder, and some brown socks with red at the heel and toe—the kind that you can get from Sears with instructions for making them into a stuffed toy monkey. I packed myself into as many layers as I could, put on a pair of gloves that I'd noticed the night before on Avery's workbench downstairs, and dragged a sack of birdseed from the back hall out to the empty feeder in the backyard. After I finished with that, I picked up the twigs and branches that had collected on the lawn and stacked them in the garage to use as kindling. Then I dragged the storm windows up from the basement, washed them in the driveway, and put them in the window frames.

I pulled the green tomatoes that were left on Avery's tomato plants from the stalks, thinking vague thoughts about chutneys and relish, and decapitated the dead flowering plants in Avery's small border garden next to the garage, wondering what I should have done to protect the garden from the frost and hearing Claire's mother's voice saying something about mulching *only* with salt-marsh hay.

The tasks were repetitive and soothing. I no longer felt like an observer at the time capsule of Avery's house, and the house felt more alive. By the time I was finished it was noon. I showered and made a sandwich, then I sorted through Avery's mail. There was a water bill and a gas credit-card bill and a notice that his mortgage company had sold its mortgage on Avery's house to someone else. There was a circular inviting "Mr. Kincair" to tour a condominium community near the Skyline Drive and collect his award of a "Personal T.V., Radar-Detecting Device, or Holiday for Two to Beautiful Gulf Coast of Mexico," and there was a solicitation from the Save the Whales Foundation. I put the bills on the pile of them that I'd been building on the bookcase, and I wondered whether I should try to get Avery's name off all those junk-mail lists or whether it would serve the companies right to have their fliers build up for years at a dead man's doorstep.

The only real letter was in a long white envelope with a typewritten return address of "R. P. Ault, Ph.D.," at Ohio University in Athens. I felt uncomfortable opening it, just as

I'd felt uncomfortable opening the couple of letters that had arrived for Avery the week before. Somewhere along the line, someone—probably Grandad—had impressed so strongly on me the wrongness of opening someone else's letters that now, as I opened Avery's, I expected to hear sirens screaming up the street.

The typewritten letter, on university letterhead, was simple:

Oct. 31

Kincaid,

I've tried to call you for two days but get no answer. Our tests confirm your findings. See chart attached. Let me know what else I can do.

Rich

There was a single-page chart paper-clipped to the letter, and the chart, or part of it, looked familiar. "Jarvis Beck," it said at the top, and spread horizontally beneath the heading were columns of numbers titled "pH," "Halogenated Aliphatic Hydrocarbons," and "Substituted Benzenes," with a vertical column of dates at the far left. Beck. Jarvis Beck. The name nagged at me. Did I know this guy? Then I remembered where I'd seen it before. This chart, or something like it, had been on one of Avery's computer disks. I assumed the lab results had something to do with an article that Avery had been working on or a course he was taking, and I made a mental note to write to Rich Ault and tell him that Avery had died.

I was on my way to the Marshall County Historical Society by one. Driving Avery's truck was starting to be enjoyable now that I knew how wide the thing was and which knobs did what. I liked sitting up high, and I liked how puny all the cars on the road seemed while I was driving it. Whistling

a few lines from "King of the Road" under my breath, I took
out the map that Sikora had drawn for me and impaled it
on the radio knob so I could see it while I drove.

Marshall is twenty miles dead north of Lisbon, which is
forty miles northwest of Darby. Although a more direct route
on a four-lane highway was available, Sikora's directions took
me on a loop to the east of Lisbon, along the Beaver River
for a while and then along a series of gently winding, climb-
ing roads that passed through farmland and the occasional
very small town.

In this part of the country, family farms are set a long
distance from the road. The farmhouses are fronted by long
aprons of lawn and sometimes a pond, the barns and silos
behind. It's hard to tell where one farmstead stops and the
next begins; there are few fences except to enclose animals,
and none of the stone walls that so tightly budget the New
England countryside.

Towns emerge without warning around the next bend or
at the crest of a hill. Some are so small they hardly merit
the name; one, called Syria, erupted and disappeared in less
time than it took me to downshift to second.

Sikora was kind to construct this route for me. I could drive
slowly enough to see the Halloween cutouts still taped to the
elementary school windows, and avoided the harassment of
tollbooths and traffic lights.

Every eight or ten miles there was an apple stand. I stopped
at a place called Agnew Family Apples, bought a bag of
McIntoshes and a pint of honey in a plastic bear with a spout
in his head, and continued my journey north, stopping to
take a picture of a faded Mail Pouch tobacco sign painted on
the side of a barn and of a trio of gleaming steel grain silos.

Even with the stop for apples, I was in Marshall by three,
and parked in the city parking lot next to the courthouse.

Marshall, the largest city in the county, used to be the heart of the Steel Valley. I had hazy memories of being taken there by my mother to shop for school clothes in a department store with a soda fountain on the first floor, and of going on a school trip to the auditorium there to see a production of *The Mikado*, but I recognized practically nothing when I locked the pickup and stepped out onto Market Street. The city had been hit by the exodus of the big steel plants in the late 1970s and hadn't yet found a way to recover. The streetfront display windows of the department store were bricked in, and a sign that said FOR RENT: 20,000 SQUARE FEET OF OFFICE SPACE stretched across the face of the building. The city had paved over what I remembered as the busiest portion of Market Street as a pedestrian mall, with built-in concrete benches that no one was sitting on and a fountain in the center that had been drained for the winter and was choked with dead leaves and litter. Following Sikora's instructions, I walked over the bridge across the river, continued up the hill, and turned right at the Presbyterian church.

Right behind the church, and separated from the street by a long, circular driveway, there was a large, dark brick building with circular turrets at either end and a porch that wrapped around three sides. A carved wooden sign saying MARSHALL COUNTY HISTORICAL SOCIETY MUSEUM AND LIBRARY swung from chains above the front entrance. There wasn't a car in the driveway, and as I approached the door, I kicked myself for not having called in advance to make sure the place was open.

But I hadn't needed to. The front door was open, and a pleasant-looking elderly woman was sitting in an old leather chair behind a table heaped with brochures. At her feet sat a space heater—an alarming-looking configuration of bright orange coils and reflective metal that looked like it would be good for roasting hot dogs. She smiled and motioned to a wooden box with a hinged lid that had a slot in it.

"It's one dollar if you're under sixteen," she said.

"And if you're not?"

"We like to ask grownups for two dollars," she said.

I wadded up a couple of dollars, shoved them into the box, and felt all grown up.

She spied my camera.

"What country are you from?" she asked.

I noticed that she was wearing a name tag and that it was upside down. It looked like it said "Mrs. Mouseman." Or maybe "Mrs. Houseman."

"I'm from America," I said.

She looked pleased. "There's a dear," she said. "The tour doesn't start until three-thirty, but we can start early, if you'd like."

I thanked her profusely, assuring her that I was very happy to take myself through the building and that I'd come back and ask her any questions that I had at the end.

I entered a long, dim, freezing room illuminated by three tear-shaped yellow glass lamps that hung from the ceiling on black metal rods. The place was packed so tightly with glass-topped display tables that my backside brushed the table behind me as I bent over to inspect what was inside the first one. It contained a gray clay sculpture of a sleeping man's face. I squinted to read the card that lay next to it, which had been typed on a manual typewriter with uneven keys, so that the *e*'s and *o*'s rode above the rest of the words.

DEATH MASK OF CHARLES ARTHUR "PRETTY BOY" FLOYD

Taken within hours after his death by shooting outside the Conkle farm on October 22, 1934. Ended a four-year spree of murder and robbery in which at least fourteen persons were killed, including six law enforcement officers. Ten thousand people viewed the body at the Sturgis Funeral Home.

The mask was very small—about the size of a box turtle. It didn't show the chin or the forehead—just his lips and his nose, which was a little longer than most men's noses, and his closed eyes. I wondered how old he'd been when he died.

I shivered in the cold, flexed my fingers, and stepped on to the next table, fighting off a wave of sadness.

Except for some framed pictures of weeping willow trees made out of dead people's hair, the rest of the museum's belongings were less morbid than the death mask. One table was crammed with small wire-rimmed eyeglasses left to the society by the family of a Marshall optician; another contained a battered set of McGuffey readers; the next held a collection of bone-colored meerschaum pipes, one shaped like a cobra, another like a man's arm, and another like an owl.

The room grew even darker, and my hands grew even colder. I could barely make out the writing on the cards attached to the glass bell display, and I couldn't find the century-old hunk of bread that Sikora had told me about.

Finally, I remembered the point of my trip to Marshall and pulled from my bag the book that Avery had borrowed. I hiked back to Mrs. Mouseman and asked what to do with it.

"Library returns are upstairs in the library, dear," she said.

She led me up a flight of stairs to another room, identical in size, shape, and dimness to the museum hall beneath it, but even colder. The walls were lined with glass-doored bookcases, and there were three mammoth oak tables in the center of the room. An elderly man sat alone at the farthest table, surrounded by books, yellow legal pads, a thermos, and a box of Ritz crackers.

Mrs. Mouseman held a finger up to her lips and whispered very loudly: "That's Judge Feld. He's working on a very important genealogy."

Judge Feld coughed.

"We mustn't disturb him," she whispered, even more loudly.

She shuffled slowly through a stack of book sign-out cards and found the one she was looking for. I could see Avery's signature, in black felt-tip pen, at the bottom of the card.

"I'm afraid Mr. Kincaid has been very tardy," she said. "I'm glad you took the matter out of his hands."

She calculated the fine on her fingertips.

"That will be seventy cents."

I scavenged in my bag for change.

She slid the card back into its pocket at the back of the book.

"The old coal mines," she said, "have been a very popular subject at the society this year. I've been thinking of asking someone from the university to come give us a lecture about them."

She placed the book on a stack on top of a file cabinet.

"Kincaid," she said, her voice ringing to the back of the hall. "Mr. Kincaid . . . and coal mining. I believe that rings a bell."

Judge Feld coughed and loudly withdrew some crackers from his box.

Mrs. Mouseman transformed her voice to a loud whisper again. A look of triumph crossed her face.

"Mr. Kincaid! Why, his photocopies are ready."

Her face darkened briefly.

"You know," she said, "it is really rather disturbing that he asked us to make the copies so quickly and he still hasn't come for them."

I decided I didn't want to broach the subject of Avery's death with a total stranger, and a nutty one at that.

"He asked me to apologize," I said.

She handed me a large yellow envelope with *To be picked up by A. Kincaid* written in Magic Marker on the front.

She calculated on her fingers again.

"That will be two dollars and forty-eight cents. We didn't charge any extra for the tape."

I counted out the money, then opened the envelope.

"They're maps of some of the old mines," she said. "He wanted to make the copies himself, but I said, 'Oh, no you don't.' We can't have just anybody handling those old maps. They'll fall to pieces. Why, just last spring somebody else was looking through this same set and tore one down the middle. So Mrs. Harvey spent an entire hour making the copies for him, and then I taped them together myself."

She walked to the door.

"It's four o'clock, and I must be going. Judge Feld will lock up if you want to stay a little longer, isn't that right, Judge Feld?"

Judge Feld made a low moan.

I took the envelope to a table and pulled out the maps. There were two of them, each copied in four different sections and taped together. They had GAITHERS COAL COMPANY printed in block letters at the lower right corner, and the date AUGUST 6, 1878. A second sheet stapled to one of the maps contained a rough diagram of what seemed to be the interior of a mine. One map appeared to be a continuation northward of the other, and I placed it above the first one on the table. I could make out what appeared to be a portion of a river or a stream cutting diagonally through the upper left quadrant, and the words JARVIS BECK lettered along it.

I tensed slightly with recognition of the words. Jarvis Beck was no graduate student or thesis adviser. Jarvis Beck was obviously a tributary of some sort. *Beck* . . . I racked my brain. Didn't it show up in the *Times* crossword puzzle every six months or so? Wasn't it a word for a stream of some kind?

What a peculiar project! Avery was researching something that had to do with this stream; he'd asked that guy at Ohio University to run tests on what—the water?—for him. And he was making some sort of connection to old coal mines. Hadn't Kevin Kogut mentioned something about Avery starting new research this summer? My memory of the conversation was a blur; I couldn't remember anything that Kevin had said about it.

I packed up the photocopies and drove back to Darby. Finding the maps Avery had been looking at unnerved me, but I couldn't put my finger on why. It had something to do with Avery's having been so obviously in the middle of things when he died. It just didn't feel right. As Sikora kept saying, how could a person as depressed as Avery must have been, if he'd killed himself, have had enough initiative to be starting a new research project—one that had him digging up old maps and talking with old friends from O.U.?

Avery's front door was unlocked. I berated myself for not having pulled it tight behind me when I left. The house was freezing, and the bulb in the overhead light in the living room burned out when I turned the switch on, so I replaced it with a bulb from the hall lamp. The furnace was on some sort of self-timing system that I couldn't make sense of, so I pushed the dial up a notch and lit a fire in the fireplace to be on the safe side. I sliced up some cheese for a toasted cheese sandwich and thought about asking Sikora over for dinner. Last night had been the nicest I'd spent with a guy in years. And that included years with Hugh. So why was I fighting him? Why didn't I get on the phone and say, Hey, Dan, get the heck over here—I'm hungry for more than Velveeta?

Instead, I got on the phone and called the Dallas house for word on Kevin. There was no answer.

I called directory information in Athens and asked for Richard Ault. I called that number, and a man with a strong southern Ohio accent answered the phone. I told him that I was Avery's sister, and that I knew he had sent Avery a letter recently, and that Avery had died last week. He asked if I would hold the line while he got on a different phone so his kids couldn't hear him. Then he asked me how Avery had died.

"The police reported it as suicide," I said.

The line was silent for a moment, then, "I'm very sorry," he said. "This must be a difficult time for you."

I told him that I appreciated his concern—a phrase I must have spoken two hundred times in the past week. I explained that I was interested in the details of one of Avery's research projects, and since I'd seen his letter to Avery, I thought he might be able to help me.

"A couple of weeks ago," he said, "Avery called me and said that he wanted me to confirm some tests that he'd run on water from a stream that he fished in sometimes. He said that he had been fishing for trout there at the beginning of the summer, the way he had for years, and for some reason there weren't any ephemerids—mayflies, that is—at a certain area of the stream. He noticed it because he likes to use a certain trout fly—a Royal Coachman, I think—that time of year, since it looks like a mayfly on the water."

Ault spoke in a slow, precise, vaguely patronizing way—a carryover from the lecture hall, I'm sure—but his voice was also tense, and I sensed a tone of genuine concern about Avery.

"Are you with me?" he said.

"Go on," I said.

"And he noticed that the part of the stream that the mayflies had disappeared from was swarming with chironomids—gnats, really—a dipteran insect."

I scribbled with a pencil stub on the inside cover of the phone book. *Royal Coachman,* I wrote. *Chironomids. Dipteran. Mayfly.*

"Why would that be?" I asked.

"Well, that was just the question Avery was asking. It seemed that something—he didn't know what—was affecting the insect balance. The larvae of mayflies are very sensitive to pollutants. That's why you usually find them in a pristine stream with native trout. Chironomids, on the other hand, are very tolerant. Avery said that he'd done some tests of the water with a field kit—at the time that he first noticed the absence of mayflies and at intervals throughout the summer. He told me that the initial tests had shown normal pH but high levels of heavy metal ions, and that the heavy metal concentrations were back to normal at the end of the summer."

"So why did he call you?" I asked.

"He called me," he said, "because during September the tests again showed high levels of the heavy metals—this time alarmingly high levels. As I recall, the zinc test was reading over one hundred parts per million, which is nearly off the scale. He was concerned about the safety of the water but worried about the reliability of his field test kit. He wanted to report his results to the state but asked me to run some tests at the lab here to substantiate his findings."

He spoke excruciatingly slowly and seemed determined not to get to the point.

I felt myself flush with frustration.

"When did he call you?"

Ault paused.

"I was in the lab when he got through to me," he said, "with Allison Gray, one of my graduate students, at her bi-weekly meeting. Which means it was on a Friday afternoon."

I could hear him flipping through the pages of a calendar.

"Yes," he said. "He called on Friday, October twenty-fourth, and said he was mailing me the samples and a report of his own results that day."

"The chart that said 'Jarvis Beck' at the top?"

"Yes."

I could smell my toasted cheese sandwich burning on the broiler.

"At the time we talked," he said, "we were simply sur-prised at the levels of the heavy metals. He asked me to run some confirming tests, and I agreed that I would. That's all.

"But," he said, "you should understand—there are report-ing requirements in a situation like this. Avery was under an obligation to report his findings to the state—which I'm sure he planned to do. In fact, now that he's dead, I suppose I'm under the same obligation. But of course he didn't want to do any reporting until he knew that his findings were valid. Nobody wants to be embarrassed by inaccurate analysis— especially not a biologist like Avery. When the levels went down during his summer tests, he became concerned that his initial findings—which were so dramatic—were flawed in some way."

While Ault spoke, I reached into the envelope containing the maps from the Historical Society, unfolded them, and laid them on the living room floor beside me.

"Rich," I said, "what *would* account for the high levels of chemicals?"

"I don't pretend to be the expert," he said.

Could have fooled me, I thought.

"But," he continued, "the contamination could have come from any number of sources. The most likely explanation was that there had been a shift in the underground springs feeding the stream, and the new source was contaminated from mine tailings. A lot of trout streams in Pennsylvania and West Virginia have been polluted from coal mines. But the pollution from the mines is usually associated with a drop in pH. We both assumed that the stream that Avery fished in must have been buffered—that is, it was able to absorb large amounts of acid without changing its pH. What was bothering Avery was the zinc. A lot of nasty things leach from coal mines, but zinc isn't usually one of them in the Midwest. That's why I ran more tests with a colleague here in the department. The water had unusually high levels of substituted benzenes and toxic hydrocarbons in addition to copper and zinc."

"Acid rain?" I asked.

I could feel his lip curling.

"Not a chance," he said. "Not with this analysis."

"Could somebody be dumping chemicals right into the stream?"

"It's possible," he said. "But it's also possible that there was a leak in some factory's waste tanks upstream, or that an old buried tank corroded and burst."

I heard a rhythmic creaking from Ault's end of the line, as though he were rocking slightly in his desk chair.

"Look," I said, "neither of us has said it, but I know that we're thinking the same thing. We're thinking that it looks like Avery may have stumbled onto the fact that somebody, somehow, was releasing toxic chemicals into the water that he was fishing in. And we're thinking that it's a pretty extraordinary coincidence that Avery happened to blow his brains out two days after he called you to ask you to confirm his findings that the chemical levels in the stream in September were alarmingly high."

"Libby," he said, "I think you're jumping the gun. If Avery had had any clear suspicions about how the heavy metals had gotten into the water at those levels, I'm sure he would have told me. But, as I already told you, he barely knew that there was a problem. In fact, he was concerned that there was something wrong with his testing methods and that the levels weren't—no, *couldn't be*—as high as they had tested for him."

I asked him if, during his conversation with Avery, Avery had mentioned anything about investigating old coal mines.

"No," he said. "No, Avery never said anything about it." And then, "As I said, Libby, I think you're jumping the gun."

"Goodbye, Rich," I said. "Thanks for your time."

I hung up. Jumping the gun, I thought. A pretty choice of words to use with the bereaved.

My toasted cheese sandwich looked like a chunk of asphalt siding. I scraped it off the broiler pan, poured some milk into one of Avery's Pittsburgh Steelers glasses, and kicked myself for not having remembered to buy some knives and forks and things to replace what had disappeared with Pam Bates.

I settled down on the living room floor next to the maps and tried to get a sense of the distances and directions they charted. It was useless. They showed an enlargement of a very small area, and the only road that was labeled—Mill-iron Road—meant nothing to me.

I went out to the truck, got Avery's county road map book, and sat on the floor with it. I ran my finger along Copper-head Creek, the ladle-shaped line that turned west off the Ohio River at the West Virginia border and dipped beneath Darby before tapering to the north. Then I traced Armstrong Road south out of the center of town, toward Copperhead Creek, for twenty miles or so to where it joined Tappan Road, a stubby, convoluted trail that edged southeast toward the river and branched out into two other roads, one of which was, to my astonishment, Milliron Road.

I compared that portion of the map to the mining map. If this Milliron Road was the same one that was on the mining map, it took a forty-five-degree descent southeast and then ran parallel along Jarvis Beck for about three quarters of a mile. I scoured that section of the road map with my eyes, trying to filter out the grid lines and the mileage notations, and suddenly the letters that formed the words "Jarvis Bk." floated to the surface—along a stream that broke off from Copperhead Creek.

I looked for a long time at the black tendril that was the stream. This was where Avery had fished all summer. There used to be mayflies here, but there weren't any this year. Avery had tested the water now and again since May. At first there were high levels of chemicals, then there weren't, and then the levels rose again. Avery wanted to know why, but even before he got verification of his test results from Rich Ault, he was dead.

He told Sikora that he wanted to find out where some old coal mines were. He'd been to the Historical Society Library to see some maps, but he didn't have copies before he died.

I went into Avery's room to take another look at the disk that had seemed so meaningless to me the week before—the one labeled *Royalco*, which had the chart in it. Now I knew a little more—that "Royalco" was Avery's shorthand for Royal Coachman, the fishing lure that started this whole mess. I opened the plastic diskette box and flipped through. *Thesis 1*, *Thesis 2*, *Thesis 3*, and *Misc.* were still there, but the *Royalco* disk wasn't. I flipped through the container again from front to back, and then from back to front. I looked under the disk drive and behind the desk, bent down to see if I had inadvertently kicked the thing under the bed. I hadn't. I cursed Pam Bates under my breath. The dishes were one thing, but how could she think Avery's research was hers?

I brushed my teeth and changed into a T-shirt. I dragged

the telephone from the living room into Avery's bedroom, got into bed, and called Dan Sikora. I let it ring twenty times, and then I called Claire, but nobody was there except my answering machine.

"Libby," I said. "This is yourself. Don't bother calling back."

The thermostat said sixty-four degrees, but the house was far colder. I piled on all the blankets I could find in Avery's closet on the bed and crawled beneath them.

10

The phone, next to my head on the bed, rang at a quarter to seven, scaring me out of my skin. It was Sikora, wanting to meet me for breakfast at a diner over by the bus station. He was, he explained, already there, reading the paper, but thought he could manage to put off ordering his eggs until I arrived.

Telling him I'd be there in half an hour, I unsnarled myself from the blankets I'd heaped on the night before.

A gray autumn rain pummeled the window over Avery's desk. My nose was stuffed, and my mouth tasted like the bottom of a fish tank.

I got out of bed and looked in the mirror hanging over the dresser. A jagged red line ran down the side of my face—the impression from a fold in the pillowcase—and my hair was flat on one side and sticking straight out on the other—what Hugh used to call my "bed head."

The radiator next to the closet kicked in with some loud clanging sounds and an occasional hiss. I wondered if I was supposed to be doing something to the furnace to keep the place from blowing up.

I scoured my mouth out, showered, pulled on my jeans, one of Avery's flannel shirts, and an army-surplus rain pon-

cho that I'd found in the back hall, and was out of the house
by five after seven.

The diner, a gleaming slice of stainless steel, glass, and
black glazed brick, sat on a corner lot across the street and
half a block down from Dingo's, where I'd left off my dad
the day of Avery's funeral. Through the blur of rain and wip-
ers of my windshield I made out the lettering that ran around
the structure's belly. MAXINE'S, it said, in yellow letters three
feet high, and then, in smaller letters set in panels along the
tops of the windows: AIR-CONDITIONED—INFRA-RED BROILING—
LADIES INVITED. A round clock rimmed in pink neon and fringed
with the words TIME TO EAT stared from the rooftop through
the misty drizzle like a bloodshot eye.

I had noticed the diner—blinds drawn and the parking lot
empty—when I'd left Dad at Dingo's, and assumed it had
fallen prey to hard times. Obviously, I'd been wrong. This
morning every booth was full and there were only two empty
stools at the counter. Sikora sat in the booth at the far end,
his head bent over the newspaper, one hand wrapped around
a thick white ceramic mug big enough to wash a sweater in.
I slid in across from him. He pushed the paper aside and
squeezed my hand.

"About time," he said. "This guy was really making me
hungry."

He gestured with his head toward the booth across the aisle,
where a man in an orange hunting vest was alternating fork-
fuls of coconut cream pie with helpings of french fries.
"Sorry," I said, my stomach writhing, and then, more sharply
than I intended, "I'm not used to these command perfor-
mances."

Sikora looked a little surprised.

Why do I always have to be such a crank? Not everybody
likes to warm up for the day with a sparring match before
breakfast. Not everybody's like Hugh.

"Sorry again," I said, and returned the squeeze. "I'm just not awake yet."

A very thin, very young-looking waitress with dark circles under her eyes and her hair caught in a barrette that said VICKY on it poured me a cup of coffee. I immediately seared the roof of my mouth with it.

Sikora ordered a Number Six. I asked for some orange juice with ice and some white toast.

Sikora frowned. "Upset stomach?"

"No," I said. "Not really. I'm just a little on edge."

On edge, I thought. On edge, all right.

I pondered where to start. The maps from the Historical Society? The phone call to Ault? The missing disk?

Maybe I was imagining things. Maybe I'd put the disk somewhere and forgotten about it. Maybe I'd put it back in the envelope backward and couldn't see the label when I looked through the box.

The unlocked door? I made a mental note to get the locks changed. Maybe I was overreacting, but Avery seemed to have let a lot of keys float around.

I rubbed some steam from the window with the back of my hand. Through the space I'd cleared I could see the door to Dingo's swing open and a man about my father's age, except fatter and wearing glasses, leave the bar and start fiddling with a parking meter. Probably looking for loose change, I thought. They were always doing that—the guys at Dingo's and places like it. Dad was always doing it too—running his finger into the mouth of every pay phone in sight, mining the occasional nickel or dime; inspecting every abandoned cigarette pack for an overlooked cigarette. Where was he, anyway? Sitting on a folding chair in the lobby of some boardinghouse in Kentucky, yucking it up about the good times that never happened?

"So what's eating you?"

Sikora was shaking pepper over his eggs. The waitress had already brought our food and I hadn't even noticed.

"Everything's eating me," I said.

I tried to find a place on the table for my coffee cup.

"Everything's eating me, but it doesn't have anything to do with you," I said.

Which was only a little bit of a lie. It was eating me that I was being sucked into an eddy of questions about Avery's death against my will. It was eating me that I wasn't taking pictures. It was eating me that I wasn't in New York. It was bad enough that Avery had died. Why couldn't I just write a check for the funeral expenses and head for home? It was eating me that I had the hots for some guy who lived seven hundred miles away from me, for crying out loud.

I drank my juice and unloaded the jelly out of the little packet onto my toast. I warmed up my hands for a while longer on my coffee mug, and then, in a low voice so as not to let anyone in the booth behind us overhear me, I told Sikora about my trip to the Historical Society and about my phone conversation with Rich Ault. I told him about the coal mine maps and how I'd found what seemed like the same area south of Darby on a current map. And I told him that Kevin Kogut had told me Avery had started some new scientific research this summer.

"And," I said, "I want to drive down to Jarvis Beck this afternoon, and I want you to come with me."

Sikora's face remained expressionless the entire time I talked. He asked no questions, made no sounds—just slowly, very slowly, ate his eggs and sopped up the yolks with his toast.

The waitress named Vicky cleared the dishes, wiped down the table, and poured us more coffee.

Sikora sat awhile longer and stared at the pattern of glitter and metallic streaks on the Formica tabletop.

"Libby," he said, "of course I'll drive down there with you, if that's what you want. But I don't think it will get us anywhere. What do you expect to see, anyway? Footprints? In the rain?"

"So do you think I should go to the police with it?" I asked.

The idea had been pestering me all morning. Wasn't I out of my league here?

Sikora scowled briefly.

"If you can pry them off the stools at Mr. Donut's," he said, and then he laughed. "Libby, the cops around here aren't interested in anything unless it involves a coffee break or a high-speed chase. Believe me, if you go to them with the information that you have, which is really just a couple of hunches and a coal mine map, they'll laugh you out of the station."

I felt wounded, and a little abandoned.

"So you think I've blown this thing up? You think I'm jumping the gun, like Ault does?"

Sikora looked surprised, and then very serious.

"I don't think you're imagining things. You know I've felt from the beginning that there was something weird about the way Avery died. But you've got to understand that to most of the world—the cops, the papers, everybody else in Darby, in fact—it's already been settled that Avery killed himself. He broke up with his girlfriend, remember? A map, a chart, a conversation that you can't remember with Kevin Kogut—face it, Libby, if that's all you have to go on, nobody will pay any attention. People, even the cops around here, don't want anything bad to happen. They don't want to hear about murders—it makes them afraid. Suicide was bad enough, but it was easier to deal with because they could blame it on some weakness in Avery. They don't have to worry about it happening to themselves—or that's what they think."

"So what am I supposed to do?" I asked. "Go home?"

The diner was practically empty now. The rain had stopped, and most of the breakfast crowd had left. Vicky was moving slowly from table to table, wiping the napkin dispensers clean, dismantling them, filling them up with napkins.

"Of course not," he said. "But what I'm saying is that you—or we, that is—are on our own on this one, at least until we get some information that will make somebody stand up and pay attention."

He pulled some bills out of his wallet and continued.

"But I can't do anything over the next couple of days. I'm going to a photo show in Columbus, and I won't be back until Friday. I've got to pack my van today and leave before evening so I can set my table up tonight."

"Fine," I said. "I'll try to interfere with your plans as little as possible."

He rolled his eyes.

"Look," he said, "I didn't say I wouldn't help. But this is a big show—I've got meetings set up with a dozen dealers. Honest—it's a big deal."

I was a little embarrassed at myself.

"I know," I said. "It's just that I feel like you're my only ally here. Now that Avery's gone, I'm a stranger in town, and I've got the creeps. There's no reason I can't go ahead and check out what's on that mine map without you."

Sikora stared in my face and shook his head gently from side to side.

"Libby," he said, "I know you're a bold sort of person and you're tough and you live in New York City and all, but you're going to have to be real careful. Do you know what I mean?"

I shrugged my shoulders. If there's one thing I've learned in my life, it's that being careful gets you nowhere.

Sikora said he had to meet somebody back at his shop in fifteen minutes. We divvied up the bill and he left, giving me a nod as he pulled out of the parking lot.

I walked over to Dingo's, which looked like an air raid shelter on the outside. On the inside it looked like a gussied-up air raid shelter. The concrete floor was covered here and there with strips of dark-red indoor-outdoor carpet, compressed like felt from wear and streaked with stains. Some of the stools at the bar were wooden, some were chrome and vinyl, and one was made out of bamboo. Mounted on the wall at the far end of the room, between the ladies' and the men's rooms, was an oil painting, as big as a refrigerator door, of a truck rolling down a highway against a pink-and-orange sunset, with real electric light bulbs set into the painted headlights.

The bartender was alone in the room, washing glasses in a sink behind the bar, his back toward me. I crossed the room and turned on the switch in the wall at the right of the painting. One headlight came on; the other didn't.

"Bad size."

It was the bartender.

"My brother made it," he said. "I can't find bulbs that size except at Sears, and Sears is closed up."

I sat on the bamboo stool and surveyed the bar. Miller and Bud on tap, a king-size bottle of Old Crow, a thirty-year-old picture of a local stripper named Eyeful Tower. An illuminated plastic clock advertising Iron City beer buzzed like a bluebottle.

I could see Dad here. Maybe not at the bar. Probably at one of the tables in the corner.

I told the bartender that Max Kincaid had some insurance proceeds to collect, and that he could get in touch with his daughter if he wanted to know more. He gave me a cardboard beer coaster, and I wrote my name and address on the back.

"Don't worry, honey," he said to me. "If there's money involved, he'll get the message. He's owed me twenty-five bucks for three years."

I drove back to Avery's, thinking I'd look at the maps some more and hoping that I'd be illuminated by a beam of knowledge from somewhere.

I fed the fish, and then the phone rang.

"Libby," said the voice. "Libby Kincaid? This is Peg, dear."

She needn't have identified herself. I recognized the husky, vacant voice immediately.

"Libby, hon," she said, "Marianne asked me to call you. Begged me to call you. They're starting a search. You know.

With dogs and everything. I told Marianne we should get a psychic. Like in the *Enquirer*. Don't you think that's a good idea?"

"Peg," I said, "has something happened? Has somebody seen Kevin?"

"Oh, no, no," she said. "Ain't nobody seen him. That's what's wrong!"

"Where are they searching?"

"Well, they're looking in some woods along the highway over by the school. That's where they found his bike."

"When did they find his bike?"

"This morning. Some kids found it before school."

"Are they at the school now? The people who are searching?"

"Oh, yes, I believe they are. Marianne left me this list of people to ask to come, and you were right there on it. I'd go too, but Marianne said I'd be more help if I stayed right here and watched little Teddy and made phone calls, like I am."

I hung up and called Sikora's shop. There was no answer. Some urgent appointment, I thought.

I pulled on an extra pair of socks, laced up a pair of Avery's hiking boots, put an extra sweater and my jacket on under Avery's rain poncho, and headed for Marshall County Regional High.

In the week that had passed since I'd driven to the school to clear out Avery's office, the landscape along the route had hardened and darkened, as if preparing for the blows of an early winter. The weekend's winds had stripped the trees of their leaves, and the morning's rain had soaked the bark black. For part of the drive, everything ahead looked like a hand-colored black-and-white photograph—black trees, pewter sky, charcoal road, white buildings—relieved only by the barest yellow tint, which was the stripe in the center of the road.

The previous week I'd hardly noticed the mile-long stretch of limestone quarries just before the Route 12 intersection;

today the immense banks of stone dominated much of the roadside.

Kids used to swim in the flooded quarries around Darby. Everybody knew that somebody's cousin or brother or something had drowned in one, everybody's parents forbade it, and everybody did it, anyway.

I went with Avery once, maybe a couple of times, when I was ten or eleven. We sat out on the gravel and stone in our bathing suits, eating bologna sandwiches, both of us too terrified to set foot in the water. Avery must have been about Kevin's age then. Taller, probably, but no tougher, and still a child.

The school building looked dark and dull against the gray sky; the tinted-glass windows were dead without the aid of the sun. As I pulled into the parking lot I could see a crowd of people milling around what looked like the gymnasium's outside entrance. There were maybe eighty or a hundred of them, most in yellow or green slickers, all wearing orange Day-Glo armbands. The lot was filled, so I parked the truck in the overflow area on the grass near the football field and made my way into the gym. Ted Dallas and the police had apparently converted the entire athletic facility into search headquarters. One corner of the gym was set up with tables and coffee percolators. A huge sign, stretched across two easels near the entrance, said TAKE OFF YOUR SHOES in red poster paint. Near it, a group of men—some of them obviously police, one of them Ted Dallas—stood around a map tacked to a bulletin board, pointing here and there and writing on clipboards. A tangle of telephone extension cords ran from some phones on the floor near the bulletin board into a hallway behind the bleachers. Vince Scannell stood near the phones, testing a walkie-talkie.

Classes seemed to be under way as usual; a bell rang as I

entered the room, and I could see a river of students moving down the hall past the interior gym doors. Some stopped in groups of five or six to peer over the makeshift rope barricade that had been erected to keep them at bay. Twenty or thirty other male students—Ted's football players, from the looks of their jackets, shoulders, and haircuts—paced the crowd, disappearing occasionally into what I assumed was the locker room. The rest of the group seemed to be composed of housewives and the occasional retirement-age father.

I took off my boots and made my way through the crowd, which, given the gravity of the subject that had drawn it together, seemed a little too festive. I headed for the refreshment area and asked a man wearing a police uniform and holding a clipboard what I could do to help.

He barely acknowledged me—just nodded his head and handed me a square of cardboard with the number 48 written on it.

"What do I do with this?" I asked.

I couldn't understand what he said.

"Excuse me—what do I do with this?"

"Read my lips," he said.

"What?"

He rolled his eyes and handed me the clipboard. I figured out that I was supposed to sign my name on the line with the number 48 next to it.

Wonderful, I thought. Nothing like making people feel like morons to inspire them to pitch in and help. I took an orange armband from a plastic trash can full of them, strapped it around my arm, and surveyed the room, looking for familiar faces.

Marianne Dallas was sitting in the first row of the bleachers, Ted's coaching jacket around her shoulders. Her hair was scraped back from her face into a ponytail, and she looked as though she'd lost ten pounds in the two days since I'd seen her. The young, dark-haired woman who had introduced herself to me after the funeral as the athletic department secretary who used to date Avery was sitting at Marianne's side, trying to get her to take a cup of coffee. Marianne caught my eye. I waved and went to her.

She reached out and took my hand with hers, which was ice cold and felt small and fragile, like a child's. Her eyes were bloodshot, and I noticed that along the part her hair was growing in brown.

"Libby," she said. "Thank you. Thank you for coming."

The dark-haired woman looked at me warily and bent toward Marianne, as if to protect her from me.

"Marianne can't talk now," she said. "She's too tired. She's talked all morning so far."

Marianne smiled weakly. I was glad that someone had assumed a position as her protector, at least for now, and told Marianne that I would talk with her later.

I found some telephones in a hall behind the bleachers and gave Sikora another try. This time he answered on the first ring. He said he needed to buy gas but that he'd come as fast as he could.

I asked a woman at the coffee table what time the search was going to start.

"As soon as they get their goddamned grid set up," she said. And then, "Excuse me—I'm just frustrated out of my mind at how long it's taking to get this thing organized. They found his bike at seven. If it were my Janice that disappeared—"

At that moment, a short, muscular man with a red crew cut stood up in the bleachers with an electronic megaphone and bellowed at the crowd.

"Searchers!" he said. "All searchers assemble in the gym!"

The crowd gravitated to the area in front of the bleachers. The man with the bullhorn identified himself as Sergeant Ryan and told us to line ourselves up by number in the field adjacent to the football field. There was a five-minute lapse

while everyone put shoes or boots back on and then headed
outside.

Once we were in the field, the sergeant, Ted at his side,
and the rest of the search coordinators lined us up at twenty-
foot intervals, starting at the edge of the highway, and ordered us to advance slowly into the fields and woods beyond
it, keeping alert for anything—a candy wrapper, a scrap of
cardboard, a piece of yarn—that might have something to
do with Kevin.

Sergeant Ryan continued to yell through his bullhorn.

"This is a team effort! Don't stop unless you absolutely
have to. By 'have to' I mean you broke your leg. If you break
your leg, send the next person in line to me and I'll arrange
a substitute."

A couple of football players ran along the line of searchers,
passing out plastic bags. For a minute I wondered if they
were for getting sick into.

"Kevin was wearing a dark-blue parka, orange hat, brown
corduroy pants, a red sweatshirt, and black-and-white high-
top sneakers when he left home on Saturday."

Marianne Dallas had been standing to one side of the sergeant with Ted, Scannell, the cop who had given me my
number, and the athletic department secretary. Now she
stepped forward to Ryan and said something. He raised the
bullhorn again.

"The sweatshirt had a hood on it, and he probably wasn't
wearing any gloves."

Marianne started to cry, and Ted put his arm around her
and led her back to the building.

"You each have a plastic bag. Whatever you find on the
search, you put in the bag. You find something that you think
is important, yell 'I have something here,' and I'll come to
you. Remember that—don't move. I'll come to *you*. I'll come
to *you* because I need to mark the exact location of the ob-
ject on the grid."

Ryan waved his clipboard in the air.

We started searching at ten-thirty and moved forward

through the field like figures in a prehistoric ritual—slowly, our eyes to the ground, silently, grimly.

The field was muddy, making it hard to walk and harder to see what was beneath our feet. The rain had turned to a fine, icy drizzle that saturated my gloves and worked its way under my hood and down the back of my neck. Every ten minutes or so, I lifted my head and focused on something in the distance—the group of grain elevators on the farmland far off to the right of the school building, or the school buses parked near the side entrance to the school—to relieve my eyes from the strain of concentration.

Twenty feet to my left was an elderly woman wearing a translucent pink plastic raincoat over a parka and one of those plastic rain bonnets that pleat up like an accordion when not in use. The same distance to my right was a young Asian woman with her hair in braids. Now and then they dipped to the ground and bobbed back up, and so did I. Sometimes we hollered the results of our search to each other, more to relieve the tension than anything else.

"Roach, gum wrapper," the Asian woman yelled, loudly enough for her immediate neighbors to hear but not sufficiently loud to draw the attention of the search leaders. "Kleenex tissue," from the woman in the pink raincoat. "Piece of a pencil."

By one o'clock I'd found a Mercury dime, a flattened hair curler, a Burger King french-fry container, the bottom part of a lipstick in a color called It's Your Mauve, an empty book of matches, and some jagged pieces of orange ceramic that looked like they might be part of a flowerpot. The shards looked dangerous, so I put them in the bag.

At two, we were still at least a hundred yards from entering the wooded area that we'd been aiming for. Ryan pumped his bullhorn up a few decibels and told us to break for half an hour—there was food in the gym.

No one had yelled "I have something here" all morning.

*   *   *

I took off my boots and turned in my plastic bag at a table staffed by Ryan and a woman cop, who told me to tie it shut and gave me a sticker to write my number on and attach to the bag. The woman held my bag up to the light to get a better view of the orange ceramic fragments.

"That's no flowerpot, honey," she said. "That's skeet, and they're not supposed to shoot it on school property. Someday one of these kids is going to get his head blown off."

I took a new plastic bag for the second leg of the search and headed for the lunch table. A cafeteria worker in a green apron handed me a packet of saltines and a white Styrofoam bowl filled with chili.

I climbed partway up into the bleachers, rubbed my hair as dry as I could with a paper napkin, and panned the crowd for Sikora. I finally caught sight of him standing by the bulletin board with the grid map on it, gesturing vigorously while he talked with Scannell.

After a while he looked up at the bleachers, caught my eye, and joined me. I gave him a cracker and asked what was going on with Scannell.

"Nothing," he said. "Which is the problem. I asked him why they were concentrating the search around here when there was a game Saturday night and a hundred people would have seen Kevin if he'd been here—either at practice in the afternoon or at the game at night."

"They found his bike here."

"Yeah, but what does that mean—that he started hitchhiking from here? That some kid stole his bike from somewhere else and left it here? If somebody abducted him by the side of the highway, it seems more likely that they'd take him off in a car than drag him across a field, lit up all night with floodlights, no less, and into the woods. Pardon my French, but these guys have got their heads stuffed where the sun don't shine."

"Okay, Mannix," I said. "What would you do to find him?"

"Well, I'd sure make a point of finding out if anybody around here saw him over the weekend. I told the guy at the

Sohio station a half mile down the road that I was coming over here to search for Kevin Kogut, and he didn't know anything about it. He said he'd been working all day and evening all weekend, and no cop ever asked him anything."

The sergeant was on his feet again, and the bleachers screeched while the crowd descended to the floor and pulled their shoes on again.

Sikora asked if I wanted to do something after he got back from the photo show. Maybe take a hike somewhere together or go see a movie. I told him yes, and then we walked off to our assigned places—me to row 48, and Sikora to a wing formed at the end of the line by latecomers to the search, who trailed a quarter of a mile behind the rest.

The afternoon was longer and harder than the morning. The woman in the pink raincoat, the Asian woman, and I no longer made any effort at conversation. Fatigue, coupled with my dispiriting conversation with Sikora, sapped me of whatever small enthusiasm for the task I'd been able to feel before lunch. The laces in my boots were completely clogged with mud, and my neck ached from the way I'd been leaning forward all day.

I found a purple pocket comb with most of the teeth missing and a small plastic He-Man figurine. Once we were in the wooded area, which ended up being a narrow section of trees that we passed through in half an hour, I found three empty cigarette packs.

I watched the woman in the pink raincoat light up a cigarette and longed for my own.

Just as the light became so dim that I couldn't tell the difference between a root and a rock, I heard a man's voice yell from off to the right, "Hey—I think I've got something! I really have something!" I looked behind me. The voice was Dan Sikora's.

I saw Dallas and the sergeant and a couple of other cops close in on him. I ran to see what he'd found, but by then the police had already bagged it and were halfway to the gym, Sikora with them. The rest of the group began to break up and drift back to the school, in spite of the voice from the bullhorn that commanded us to continue searching.

Testy, cold, and tired, we moved into the building. I yanked off my boots and made my way over to the table in front of the grid, where most of the crowd had collected. The chatter was loud and tense.

Sikora moved toward me with two cups of coffee. He looked pale and shaken.

"So what was it?" I said. "What did you find?"

"Look for yourself," he said.

Sergeant Ryan was handing a plastic bag to a woman officer seated at a table. She reached inside and pulled out what looked like a handful of small pieces of cardboard.

"It's his library card," somebody said.

The objects were damp at the edges and clung together.

The policewoman peeled them apart and laid them in front of her, side by side.

First, the library card. Then a Red Cross lifesaving certificate. And then the picture of Avery that I had given to Kevin in Avery's office the week before.

Sikora grabbed my arm.

"Jesus, Libby," he said. "I thought it was just part of a candy-bar wrapper or something until I turned it over. I hope it doesn't mean—"

"That somebody took his wallet from him? That he was in a struggle with someone?"

He closed his eyes and shook his head.

I put my arm around him. "Maybe they fell out of his pocket," I said. "Maybe he just dropped them on his way home from school."

We made our way to the door as Vince Scannell took to the bleachers with the megaphone.

"Thank you all for your effort!" he yelled. "No speeding in the parking lot!"

11

I stopped at a Phar-Mor drugstore a quarter of a mile away from the school and bought some Ben-Gay for my neck and some supplies for my cold—Sudafeds, cough drops, and a "man-size" box of tissues with pictures of the Wild West printed all over it. I bought a copy of *Americans*, which had a picture of Bruce Springsteen's face on the cover that made him look like the leader of the free world. I also bought a copy of the competition, which had a picture of Bruce Springsteen on the cover that made him look like Christ crucified, standing on a backlit stage with his arms out at his sides and his head slumped into his chest.

I ordered a burger and a root beer at the drive-in window at Little Gene's Root Beer stand, next to the Phar-Mor. A signed taped to the window warranted that the stand was staffed by Marshall County Regional High School voc-ed students "Who are Advancing Their Careers in Restaurant Science Under the Sponsorship of the Marshall County Junior Chamber of Commerce." My student waitress advanced her career just fine, except she didn't give me any napkins and my root beer was flat.

I flipped through the *Americans* Springsteen feature at a long red light.

Damn. Why didn't I get this Springsteen stint? Octavia knows it would have been perfect for me.

I didn't even know it was in the works.

I tilted the first page of the article sideways and looked at the photo credits.

"E. Neil Whitlow," it said.

E. Neil Whitlow? E. Neil Whitlow? Is this some kind of joke? There is no E. Neil Whitlow.

I balanced the open magazine on top of the burger in my lap and looked at the pictures again.

All over the place: "E. Neil Whitlow."

"Eddy Whitlow?" I hollered it out loud.

I couldn't believe it. That little smart-mouth intern from Bennington or Sarah Lawrence or one of those places that guys aren't supposed to go to? The one with the fifteen-hundred-dollar cowboy boots and the twenty-pound Nikon? The one who broke my light meter and didn't pay to fix it?

I pounded the steering wheel with both hands. My ears were burning. I couldn't breathe. I popped two Sudafeds and washed them down with the so-called root beer.

Octavia! How could you do this to me?

What's going on? Is he sleeping with her?

E. Neil Whitlow.

I could have strangled him with his hand-crafted bolo tie. Stuffed him into his snakeskin camera case.

Lucas scratched at the door and whimpered while I un-locked it from the outside. Some watchdog, I thought. He's begging me to come in.

And damn. I forgot to get the locks changed. I wedged a kitchen chair under the front-door knob and turned my at-tention to Lucas, who was leaning against the backs of my legs, panting and wagging his tail. I checked his wound, which wasn't seeping but still looked awful—it had turned from red to a purple-pink, and the fur was starting to grow back where Pam had shaved it away. Poor fellow; it looked like it itched something fierce.

He seemed to have used the dog door just fine. The newspapers that I'd spread in front of it were covered with muddy pawprints, as was the rug in the hallway next to the kitchen.

I fed him some dog food in the kitchen, put fresh water in his water bowl, and cleaned up the hall. I shut the storm door over the dog door and wedged a kitchen chair under the knob on the inside door.

There was nothing interesting in Avery's mail today, except an extravagant mail order catalog from a fishing-supply company. I flipped through it while I took a bath, marveling at the names of the flies. Gold Monkey, Esmeralda, Amber Nymph. They sounded like cocktails, or exotic dancers. Ginger Palmer, Dixie Devil, Bouncer, Parmachenie Beau.

My cold was packing a wallop. I smeared some Ben-Gay on my neck and shoulders, gave Lucas a good-night muzzle rub, blew my nose, and sank into immediate sleep.

Lucas was growling. I don't know how long he'd been at it. I was sleeping heavily, and it took me a while to surface.

Lucas was growling, and the room was pitch black except for the glow-in-the-dark dial on Avery's alarm clock, which said 2:32 A.M. I heard a footstep on the gravel driveway next to the bedroom wall, and then another, and then a long pause while I thought that maybe I was imagining things or I was dreaming or there was a raccoon out there or a trash can rolling around. Lucas growled again, and I turned on the bedroom light, and then the footsteps ran down the drive, or maybe across the drive and onto the lawn, because I heard only five or six steps grinding the gravel. Then I looked out the bedroom window at the driveway and the front lawn and I saw the beam of a flashlight for a second or two seconds, or maybe it was three, and some kind of figure attached to

the flashlight—just the shadow of a figure—disappear behind the spruce trees down by the street. That was all I saw
and all I heard.

And that was what I told the cops when they finally came
a half hour later, and no, I couldn't tell if it was a man or a
woman, and no, I couldn't say how tall he or she was. I just
knew it was a person, that's all, and the person had a flashlight, and no, I didn't hear any car.

The two officers looked around outside and then came inside. One was a tall, thin, pale man with short blond hair,
gray-tinted eyeglasses, and a big pink birthmark that started
in the middle of his right cheek and went down into his collar. He looked a little familiar, but I didn't know why. Maybe
I went to elementary school with him.

Whippo, he said his name was. Officer Whippo. He was
sorry about my brother, he said. He spoke in a soft, high-
pitched voice that was oddly soothing. He didn't know Avery, he said—just knew who he was. Lucas lumbered over to
him, and Whippo stroked him on the neck.

His colleague was fatter, cruder, abrasive. He had black
hair and long, skinny sideburns. He didn't take his hat off
and didn't tell me his name. He said he saw me at the search
for Kevin Kogut by the school. He said he was wondering
why I was staying in town so long after Avery died and why
I was looking for Kevin.

I said I was taking care of Avery's estate and that the Dallases had been friends of Avery's, so I thought I should help
them.

He rolled his eyes.

"The sounds that you think you heard," he said. "How do
you know they weren't a dog?"

"Because they were human footsteps, and because I saw
somebody with a flashlight."

"Could that flashlight have been the headlight of a car?"

"If it was a very small car, with headlights about two inches
in diameter."

He took a step forward—to scare me, I guess.

It worked. I stepped back.

Officer Whippo piped up, "Aw, come on, Duane. Leave her alone."

Duane stepped forward again and looked me straight in the face from a distance of about six inches—the way Sergeant Carter used to look into Gomer Pyle's face when he was chewing him out.

"You seem a little wasted, Miss Kincaid," he said. "A little bit like you've been at the party too long."

He was referring to my eyes, which, if they looked anything like they did when I went to bed, were pink and bleary.

"I have a terrible cold," I said. And I hope you get it, I didn't say.

"Sure you do," he said, and went back out to the patrol car.

Officer Whippo stayed awhile longer, checking the locks on the windows, poking around the basement and in the closets. I sat on the sofa, wrapped in a blanket, my feet burrowed in Avery's moccasins, which were about four inches too long for me.

"You might," Whippo said, "ask someone to come spend the rest of the night with you. And maybe tomorrow night. Or maybe you could go spend some time with some friends."

I wondered if this was an obliquely worded proposition, then remembered my bloodshot eyes and Avery's slippers. Definitely not.

I thanked him and stood up to see him to the door.

"That's not a bad idea," I said.

"You don't have any idea who was trying to get in, do you?" he asked. "I mean—do you have an old boyfriend who's mad about something? A husband or something? That happens sometimes, you know."

"I wish I did," I said. "Know who was creeping around, that is."

"Any crank phone calls?"

"No. But I was meaning to tell you before your friend started beating up on me that when I got in yesterday the front door was unlocked, and I thought that maybe I forgot to lock it when I went out—which is unlikely."

"Did you change the locks?"

"No. I was going to today, but I forgot."

"You ought to change the locks, miss," he said.

"I'm going to," I said.

I thought of telling him about the disk that was missing.

"Do you have a gun?" he said.

"A what?"

"A gun. Do you know how to use a gun?"

"My brother had a gun," I said.

"I know," he said. "I saw it. I'm sorry."

"You saw it?"

"It. Him. Everything. I was at the scene."

"You saw Avery . . . dead?" I asked.

"That's right, miss."

"Avery? And the blood? And the dog?"

"Yes, miss. I took him to the clinic. The dog, that is. Your brother . . ."

"My brother couldn't be helped."

"That's right. He couldn't be helped."

I was feeling light-headed, and my ears started to ring.

"Are you all right?" he asked.

I sat down.

"I'm all right," I said.

I heard the patrol car engine start up, and the headlights suddenly shone up the driveway. Whippo buttoned up his jacket and put on his hat.

"Officer Whippo," I said. "Did it look like a suicide to you?"

He looked puzzled for a moment, then changed the look to a sad, sympathetic expression.

"Couldn't be anything else," he said. "I know sometimes you wonder, but this one . . . couldn't be anything else. No signs of an intruder or a struggle, and the gun was registered in his name. He had a real bad time with that girlfriend of his, you know. The principal at the high school says he took it real hard. He says it sent him around the bend."

He stepped out the door.

"Then there was the note," he said.

"What note?"

"The note that was on his computer."

"I don't know anything about any note that was on his computer."

Whippo dropped his eyes to the ground, as though he were embarrassed about something.

"When we got here," he said, "there was a note on his computer screen."

"What did it say?"

"It said, 'I couldn't live without her,' or 'I can't live without you,' or something like that."

"That's all? Can you give me a copy of what it said? Why didn't you guys give me a copy?"

"It disappeared," he said.

"What do you mean—'It disappeared'?"

He took a step backward, as though he were about to escape to the cruiser.

"It was my fault," he said. "I'm sorry. We were all standing around the computer, and I tripped over the cord. The whole screen went black. That is, there was a big flash, and then it turned black. I'm not used to being around computers. I'm sorry."

"And now you guys just sort of remember what it said."

"That's right," he said. "I'm sorry. I'm sorry about Duane too. He's sort of stressed out."

It pretty well explained the "Note" that was indexed but missing from Avery's disk. But if Avery killed himself, why was the "Royalco" disk missing? Why was somebody prowling around the house?

I didn't want to make Whippo apologize again.

"Thanks," I said. "Good night."

It was four-thirty. I jammed the kitchen chair underneath the doorknob again and made sure all the drapes were closed.

I got out Avery's disk box. I put the "Misc." disk into the drive and pulled up the "Note" document again. It was empty again. Maybe he'd written two notes—or a series of notes. I scoured the index for another 10/26 entry, but there wasn't one. I slammed the disk back into the box.

Lucas fell asleep again, but I couldn't. My ears were aching from my cold, and the events of the day and night buzzed in my head like flies in a jar. I called Sikora's number—once, twice, then a third time. No answer. What *is* this guy—a werewolf? Damn. I knew it. He was with Pam Bates. I thought about calling there and then got hold of myself. Idiot. He told you he'd be in Columbus tonight.

I lay on the bed and tried to tell myself to relax, to take deep breaths. Which of course I couldn't do. Somebody had been creeping around the house. Somebody had a key to this place. Somebody got in yesterday and could get in today too. Somebody came back when I was home. In the middle of the night. I longed for Canal Street and the police lock and the grates welded to the window frames.

I turned on the TV and every light in the house. I looked for the "Royalco" disk again. In the disk box, under the terminal, under the disk drive, under the bed, under the rug, on the dresser, under the dresser, in the bathroom. So somebody took it. Somebody who didn't know that Avery sent the information on it to Rich Ault. Somebody who needed that information to do something. Or to hide something.

And who says anybody had to have a key to get in? The lock had a single bolt, and the gap between the door and the frame was an eighth of an inch wide. I could probably pick it myself with a charge card in less than three seconds. Heck, I thought, if whoever it was were small enough, he could climb through the dog door.

Lucas moaned in his sleep, and I let out a yell. I scuffled into the kitchen, poured myself some orange juice, took another Sudafed, and lay down on the sofa.

Avery's picture. How did Kevin's wallet—not even Kevin's wallet: a few items from Kevin's wallet—end up in that patch of woods behind the school? The woman cop had laid the cards and the picture side by side on the table. You could read Kevin's signature on the library card and the Red Cross card as plain as could be. But it had been raining all day. It didn't seem right. Nothing seemed right.

I looked out the living room window at the place where I had seen the flashlight and whoever had been carrying it. I hadn't heard a car—at least not immediately, I hadn't. But I hadn't thought to listen, either. I'd been too scared.

Whoever it was could have run from the spruce trees to the drainage ditch that ran along Garfield Road and crept along that to a parked car at the end of the road. The night was dark. There were no streetlights. It would be easy.

Or he could have stayed in the spruce trees, waited until he thought the coast was clear, and edged back up the far side of Avery's driveway, shielded by the juniper hedge. He could have made his way to the orchard next door. Why hadn't the cops looked there?

He could have made his way to the orchard next door and waited there until he saw that the cops had gone, and then he could have come right back here.

I tried to remember if there was an outside entrance to the basement, and hoped there wasn't.

It was five-thirty. I started a pot of coffee going on the stove, changed into jeans and a sweater, and fished in Avery's dresser for more wool socks. Lucas woke up and started to act nervous, as if he was afraid that I was going to leave him again. I fed him, poured the coffee into a thermos, gathered up the mine maps and Avery's road maps, and herded us out the front door, which I carefully locked behind me.

I half expected to see someone with a hatchet in his hand sitting in the passenger seat of Avery's truck. Nobody was. I gave Lucas a boost into the seat, turned on the heater and the headlights, and headed for Jarvis Beck.

12

I decided against chancing the back roads on Avery's map—which, according to the copyright, was at least eleven years old—and headed instead into the center of town, where I knew I could pick up Armstrong Road and drive straight south. I glanced at Time Travel as I drove up Central Street and over the bridge. The daylight was so dim that I could make out only the white-and-orange CLOSED sign propped up in the window next to what looked like a crystal ball; the shades were drawn upstairs, and the lights were off.

Lucas seemed glad to be out—glad to be going somewhere. He tried sitting in the seat for a while but lost his balance too many times when I pulled around corners, and after a while he decided to lie on the seat, his nose at my hip.

Except for a newspaper delivery car that we trailed for a while, and a dairy tanker truck that trailed us for a while, we were the only travelers on Armstrong Road. The lights were on in the farmhouses, but nowhere else.

My nerves were so raw that I couldn't stand to turn the radio on; my jaw was so tight that I could barely force the rim of Avery's travel mug between my teeth.

I stroked Lucas's head and rubbed my knuckle on the top of his nose, which he seemed to like. I remembered an article that I'd seen in a Science Times section of the *New York Times*—something about how having pets can keep your blood pressure in line.

"Hey, Luke," I said. "Let's see if you can keep me from stroking out."

The huge early-morning sky was dark lavender, and pinker along the horizon. It seemed chalky and opaque, the way a color photograph prints on matte-finish paper.

We drove past the dark outlines of a Christmas tree farm, a lake with fishing cabins all around it, and a trailer park called Medina Breezes. Ten miles out of Darby we drove past the StarScape drive-in movie theater—or what used to be the StarScape. I remembered seeing *Mutiny on the Bounty* there and something with Hayley Mills in it. *The Parent Trap* maybe. Someone had pried the lettering from the back of the screen and replaced it with a plastic billboard-sized sign with movable letters. USED CARS, it said, and ANTIQUES COLLECTIBLES AUCTION SAT 11:00 TO 5:30.

I thought about taking a picture, but the light wasn't right and I was too distracted. As I glanced in the rearview mirror a blue van crossed through the intersection behind me. I could have sworn it was Dan Sikora's, with its black side door, but I dismissed the idea. He was out of town, and it was still dark enough out that black, blue, and brown all looked more or less the same. I had a buzz on from too little sleep and too much coffee. If I didn't watch out, I'd be seeing the guy behind every tree.

After about forty minutes, Tappan Road intersected Armstrong Road exactly where Avery's map said it should. I turned left and ran into a small cluster of sagging, asphalt-sided houses, one of which had a sign in the front window that said GLAMORAMA BEAUTY SALON, and a small, ancient, yellow-brick gas station—the kind with an awning over the pumps to keep everyone dry. A sign mounted on one of the supporting posts said YANNIS'S BEER, GAS, AND GROCERIES. I pulled up under the awning, turned off the motor, and waited

for someone to come fill up the tank. When nobody did, I
helped Lucas out of the truck, walked into the building, and
hollered for help.

I was about to walk out again when someone opened the
building's back door and stepped inside. It was an extremely
short, thick-waisted person, somewhere between fifty and sixty
years of age, with gray hair in a longish crew cut, wearing
brown polyester trousers—the kind that Maytag issues to its
appliance repairpeople—a wide brown leather belt, and a red
sweatshirt with a hood. The voice that came out was clearly
a woman's, but raspy and deep.

"What do you need?" she asked.

"I need a tank of gas," I said. "And some directions."

She walked out to the truck and filled it up. I stayed in the
station to look for something to eat, and settled on two small,
mealy-looking apples, some cough drops, and a box of Pop-
Tarts—the kind without the icing on top.

She came back into the station. While she was ringing up
my bill, someone else entered the building through the back
door—a heavy, middle-aged woman, also wearing a red
sweatshirt with a hood. She clearly had Down's syndrome
and was clearly related to the woman ringing up my bill.

"Hello," she said.

"Hello," I said.

The woman at the cash register looked up at me.

"My sister," she said. And then, "Jean Louise, don't you
dare do another thing until you feed them cats."

Jean Louise kicked the front door open and disappeared
around the corner of the building.

Lucas started barking by the truck. The woman snapped
open a paper bag, put my purchases inside, and looked at
me.

"I can't help seeing," she said, "that you're driving Avery
Kincaid's truck and you have his dog."

I flushed with a sudden sense of panic, although I didn't
really know why. Except that I had spent the morning feeling that by driving away from Darby I could recapture the

feeling of anonymity that I'd had a week ago, before I'd found the maps, and the letter from Ault, and before last night. I toyed with the idea of pretending that I didn't know what she was talking about—about remarking on the coincidence of my having a dog and a truck like someone's she knew.

"Where's he been?" she asked. "I haven't seen him around here since September."

I tried to get it out as fast as I could.

"He's dead," I said. "He had a terrible accident, and he died."

She was sensitive enough not to push for details. Or maybe she just wasn't interested. I couldn't tell. She shuffled the paper bags into a stack and stuffed them between the counter and the wall. Then she walked out from behind the counter and sat on a stool by the front door, in front of a display of car air-fresheners shaped like little pine trees.

"I'm sorry to hear that," she said. "Sorry indeed. He used to buy bait from me, when I had bait."

She saw that I had the road map in my hand.

"Where are you trying to get to?"

I told her that I was going fishing. That I wanted to fish down here where Avery used to fish, and that I thought the place was called Jarvis Beck.

"Jarvis Beck?" she said. "I don't know if I can get you to any Jarvis Beck, but I can get you down the road Kincaid used to take when he was looking to fish."

I told her that would help.

She took a paper bag and a chewed-up pencil and started drawing. When she ran out of room on the front, she turned the bag over and continued on the back. She narrated as she drew.

"Whatever you do, don't turn up Axelson Road. Axelson's got a pack of dogs that'll tear your arms off. There'll be the dump here on your left, and then down the road some more, and then a big blue garage-type building on your right. Then your first right after that, and then you'll have to get out of your truck and lift up the chain and the No Trespassers sign.

Then it's just that old dirt road all the way, but watch out for the mud."

She showed me where to park the truck and where to start hiking into the woods. Then she reached into a bin for some dog biscuits and put them in the bag that had the map on it.

"My mama was widowed twice before she was twenty-five," she said. "Paddled her own canoe ever since, she always said."

The back door opened again and Jean Louise came inside, holding a huge, drooling yellow cat, the kind with paws shaped like mittens.

"Jean Louise, I told you a million times to keep that thing out of here!"

I decided not to explain that I wasn't Avery's widow, thanked her for the map, and got back in the truck.

The directions on the grocery bag took me down a succession of narrow roads, each rougher and steeper than the last. The dump that the woman had referred to was a ravine crammed with banished household appliances—washing machines with the lids ripped off, gutted Frigidaires, disembowled vacuum cleaners—and broken toys: a Sting-Ray bicycle without any wheels, a rusted, crumpled jungle gym, a turtle-shaped plastic wading pool with a gash down the center. Across the road and a half mile down from the dump, I drove past the blue garage building that she'd told me about—a windowless, corrugated-metal structure with a padlock on the front door and traces of election posters clinging to the sides.

Once we'd gone past the blue building, Lucas sat up high in the seat, pawed at the dashboard, and wagged his tail, obviously recognizing the route, and obviously pleased to be near our destination. As I pulled up to the mouth of the road blocked off by the chain and the No Trespassers sign, he went into a frenzy of delight, barking and trying to run around in a circle on the seat. I got out of the truck, unfastened the chain, drove onto the road, got out again, fastened the chain behind me, and returned to the truck.

The road was lumpy with rocks and ruts and slick with mud. Lucas and I bounced around inside the truck for a couple of minutes and then came to an abrupt stop in a place that someone had cleared of trees just enough so that a car could turn around and head back out. There was another No Trespassers sign here, but this one was nailed to a tree and had bullet holes in it. I wondered for a minute if it was hunting season and wished that I had something orange to wear.

I gave Lucas a biscuit and let him out of the truck. He barked a few times, then ran—as best he could—down a path into the woods. I called after him, but stopped. He seemed so familiar with the place, I knew he wouldn't get lost.

I poured myself another cup of coffee from the thermos and spread the road map and the mine map across the hood of the truck. After I'd taken a look at Avery's fishing spot, I wanted to find Milliron Road—the only named road on the mine map. I should have asked the woman at the gas station where it was. Still, it looked easy enough to find. If I retraced my drive back to Tappan Road and took the first fork to the left instead of to the right, Milliron Road should cut in a quarter of a mile or a half mile later from the left.

I put the maps back in the car and took the path Lucas had taken. The trees, mostly oaks and maples, were tall and healthy-looking, and the black dirt beneath my boots smelled dank and rich. I picked up some dead leaves as I walked—a huge, thick, waxy yellow leaf from a tulip poplar, blunt across the top and lobed at the sides; a small, perfect, dappled orange-and-yellow maple leaf; a brittle brown oak leaf with an acorn attached.

I came to the stream almost immediately and saw Lucas sitting on a point in the bank that jutted out five or six feet into the water—a miniature peninsula shaded by some birch trees. I joined him and sat on a stump in the center of the enclave.

The only sound was the sweeping of the water as it ran

around the rocks in the stream and brushed the roots and leaves that lined the bank. I lay on my back and looked up. A silvery ribbon of sky ran behind the tree branches that fanned toward each other from either side of the water. I loaded my camera and took some pictures of the branches against the sky, some with the leaves still attached, others bare. They looked like fancy ironwork, sinuous and jet black.

A fish broke the surface of the water with a small, crisp splashing sound, then leapt a second time. I sat up. Lucas didn't make a noise or movement; he just leaned hard against my legs and looked out over the water. Avery must have taught him this—to stay quiet on the bank or in the boat so the fish wouldn't know he was there. We had learned that from fishing with Grandad: "Quiet. Don't even whisper. We don't want to scare the fish."

Lucas lay down with his head in my lap. I put my arm around him, then buried my face in his side.

"Good boy, Lucas," I said. "What a good dog you are."

After the events of the night it seemed as though I had stumbled on the most peaceful place on earth. No radios, no litter, no taxis. Just leaves, stones, the rush of water, and clean, cool air. I tried to think of a place in Manhattan where I felt this tranquil and unencumbered. The closest I could come was the ladies' room at the New York Public Library.

I closed my eyes—briefly, I thought—and drifted off, breathing the scents of the water and damp dog fur, the morning sun warm against the back of my neck. Ten, maybe fifteen minutes later, the sound of a gunshot, and then another, ripped through the air. Lucas barked and scrambled to his legs, then limped down to the water's edge, whimpering painfully all the while. I followed him and tried to comfort him, but he shook me off, still whimpering and pacing. Then another shot rang out, and Lucas leapt into the air with a piercing, horrible howl. I thought for a moment that he'd been shot, and ran toward him to look for the wound. There was no blood that I could see, but again he wouldn't let me touch him, and I couldn't be sure.

He stood still with his front leg in the water, staring across at the opposite bank—the direction that the shots seemed to have come from—snarling and trembling and appearing to be in terrible pain.

I shouted across the water: "Who's there? Who's there? What do you want?" but saw no one and heard no answer.

Lucas continued to growl. I took him by the collar and tried to drag him away from the water, but I was no match for his intensity. We stayed, frozen in that position, for what seemed like an eternity, waiting for the next shot—me crouched at Lucas's side, pulling at his collar with all my strength, desperate to drag him back to the truck but terrified to move lest I make myself a more visible target, and Lucas, every muscle in his body obsessed with holding his ground.

But the next shot never came, and no one came walking toward us through the woods. Lucas's growls turned into sporadic whimpers, and I felt his body gradually relax beneath my grip.

"Lucas," I whispered to him. "Lucas, you're a good boy, and we're going to go back to the truck now. You're scared, and so am I, but we're going to go back to the truck."

My heart decelerated, but I could still feel the occasional wild thump—like a tennis shoe banging around in a clothes dryer.

"Lucas," I said, as much to calm myself as him. "Lucas, everything will be okay as soon as we get in the truck."

I stood up and slowly steered Lucas back down the path, trying to walk quietly, trying to convince myself that nothing very frightening had happened.

"Hunters," I said to myself. "Of course, it's hunting season. Or target practice. Somebody two miles away is shooting at targets in a field, and the wind made it sound so close."

I opened the truck door and boosted Lucas up onto the seat. I locked all the doors, and then I ran my hands all over the dog, looking for a wound. Nothing.

I made an impossible three-point turn and pulled back onto

the road, scanning the woods around us the entire time for someone with a gun.

"Or a truck backfired," I said out loud. "A truck backfired, and the wind carried it here."

How could anyone know I was here? Could whoever was sneaking around Avery's house last night really have followed me? Hidden out in the orchard next door, waited for me to leave the house, and followed me? Where was he hiding his car?

My left front tire sank into a muddy rut. The rear wheels spun, and I felt a surge of panic spread from my stomach to my chest. Then, miraculously, the truck lifted out of the rut and back on the road.

"Atta girl," I said, patting the dash. "You can do it."

I continued through the mud and rocks, threading the truck around the pits, avoiding the edge of the road, talking out loud as I drove.

"We're out of here, Lucas. We're out of here but good. Two more minutes and we'll be back on the asphalt."

My knees shook as I climbed out of the truck and unfastened the chain at the bottom of the road. I noticed that this time the No Trespassers sign that swung from the center of the chain had bullet holes in it, just like the one by the water. I drove through, got out again, and fastened the chain behind me.

The road curved sharply to the left just before it joined with the main, paved road. I pulled out of the curve and came face-to-face with a red station wagon, its windows tinted, that blocked the entrance to the road. There was a gun rack on the top of the car, a man wearing sunglasses at the wheel, and a second man leaning against the driver's door, wiping the shaft of his rifle with a rag. The guy with the gun was wearing an orange vest with what looked like his hunting license clipped to the front, camouflage pants, and an orange hunting hat pulled down low over his brow.

So there were hunters after all.

They pretended not to notice me for a while. Then the guy

with the orange hat walked up to my window, carrying his rifle. Lucas bared his teeth, snarled, threw himself over my lap, and lunged at the window. I cranked it down an inch, so whoever he was could get the full effect of Lucas's growls.

The man backed off and gestured with his thumb. The guy in the car gunned the motor and slammed into reverse. I waved and pulled onto the hardtop road, with Lucas barking and clawing at the back window.

Why hadn't it occurred to me at the water? Lucas was terrified of guns—the look and sound of them—because somebody had shot him and Avery with one.

I gave him a biscuit and tried to talk him down again.

"Hey, Lucas. You're okay, Lucas. Nobody's going to hurt you. They're gone, old boy. Everything's all right."

A phobia about guns. That's all that was going on back there. Nobody was trying to kill me.

I hoped.

I reversed my route and looked for Milliron Road. According to the map, I was supposed to take a left at the first fork, and I did. And then Milliron Road was supposed to cut in from the left. But it didn't.

A quarter mile, a half mile, a mile, two miles . . . the numbers skidded by on the odometer. No road. No sign of a road. I made a U-turn and tried again, but there was no road. Two driveways and a boarded-up frozen custard stand, but no Milliron Road.

Three miles later, I was at the intersection of something called Route 9A and Tappan Road. According to my map, if I turned right, after a while I'd be back at Yannis's Beer, Gas, and Groceries and could ask the woman there to steer me to Milliron Road.

I pulled up under the awning and walked into the station. A skinny boy of about fourteen was squatting on the floor, ripping open boxes of beer and shoving the cans into the refrigerator. He didn't look up.

"Excuse me," I said. "Is the woman who was here this morning around somewhere?"

He didn't answer.

"Excuse me," I said.

He flattened the boxes, put them on top of the refrigerator, and turned to me. He had a beautiful, wide baby face violated by a thin, crescent-shaped scar that ran from his right temple to the corner of his mouth. I shuddered and tried not to stare.

"That's my mom," he said. "That's my mom who was here. She's out, and she won't be back till supper."

I pulled out my map and showed him the road we were on, and the short black thread that was labeled "Milliron Road."

"I'm trying to get to this road," I said. "It goes down by some old coal mines."

He took the map and studied it for a while, then carried it to the window and looked at it some more.

"I don't think there is such a road," he said. "It doesn't look like any road I've ever been on."

"How about the coal mines?" I asked.

"Coal mines?" he said. "Oh, yeah, there's old coal mines around here. That's what they say."

"Do you know where they are?"

He pursed his lips, looked back at the map, and pointed to the area around Milliron Road.

"Down around here," he said, "I think."

"Can you tell me how to get to them?"

"Nope," he said, "not me. I never saw them myself."

"Thanks," I said.

I let Lucas out of the truck and gave him some water from a hose at the side of the station. His legs shook as he walked across the asphalt, and I had to all but lift him back into the truck. Pam Bates had said he was in good shape, but the episode back by the stream had obviously sent him into a tailspin. I felt terrible.

"I'm sorry, Lucas," I said. "I didn't know what was going

to happen back there. Don't you worry, fellow. No more adventures for you today."

I gave him a biscuit, rubbed his neck, and pulled back out onto Tappan Road.

My sleepless night was catching up with me, and so was my cold. I poured myself another cup of coffee, tepid by this time, rolled down the car windows in hope that the cool air would shake me up a little, and headed back to Darby.

I stopped at the hardware store on Central Street, looked for new locks for Avery's house, and settled on two tough-looking dead bolts. I brought the locksmith back to the house with me, and he had them in place in fifteen minutes. It occurred to me that anyone who wanted to could break the glass in the back-door window, reach inside, and unlock the door. It also occurred to me that anyone who wanted to could break any of the dozen or so windows, climb in, and murder me in no time flat.

I asked the locksmith how hard it would be to put grates on the windows, and he looked at me blankly, as though he thought he hadn't heard me right.

"Grates," I said. "You know, like bars over the windows."

"Bars over the windows? In a house?"

"Right," I said.

"Like in a jail?"

"Not really like in a jail. To keep people out—not to keep them in."

"Lady," he said, "people don't do that around here."

He looked at me with such a worried, grave expression that tears came to my eyes.

"Are you okay?" he said.

"I'm okay," I said. "I've just got a cold."

I fed Lucas and the fish, tried to take a nap but couldn't, and decided to work off some of my nerves on a trip into town.

I bought some socks for me and a polka-dotted shower cap for Claire at the five-and-dime by Dan Sikora's, and sat in an orange plastic booth and ate a hunk of something called "peanut butter pie" at a place called Family Faire a block away. Then I sat for a long time on a stone bench built into a nook on the Central Street bridge, thinking about Avery and the research he'd done at the stream, and what the mines had to do with it, and who would have killed him. And I got nowhere.

I took some pictures, which usually makes me feel better but didn't this time. I bought a few frozen dinners and a *Marshall Post-Gazette* at the 7-Eleven, drove back to Avery's, and spent the rest of the afternoon and evening puttering around—watching television, looking through Avery's books, making phone calls. I called Claire and she wasn't there. I called Uncle Garth and he wasn't there. I knew Dan Sikora wasn't there, but I called him anyway and he wasn't there, either.

I washed out the refrigerator and vacuumed the rugs and sorted through Avery's clothes. I made a pile of sweaters and shirts that I could wear and a pile of trousers, belts, shoes, and pajamas that I couldn't, for Goodwill. I set Avery's neckties aside to give to Ted Dallas, and I folded up a green flannel bathrobe that I thought might fit Sikora.

I dragged up some empty cardboard boxes from the basement and filled them with things from Avery's bureau and desk. Nail clippers; a shallow leather box with his birth certificate, an expired passport, and a two-dollar bill inside; a small china dish that said BLUE HOLE, CASTALIA, OHIO on it and had a picture of a bright-blue lake in the center; a roll of quarters; a roll of pennies; a John F. Kennedy half-dollar; a broken wristwatch; and a photograph of our mother when she graduated from nursing school, her lips and cheeks delicately rouged by a skilled photographer's colorist, her hair in an immaculately permed pageboy, her face proud and happy.

Lucas, asleep in his dog bed, gave an unconscious growl

and a yelp, scaring me out of my wits. I switched on all the lights and turned on the television. The TV section of the newspaper said I could choose from *The Birds*, *Bunny Lake Is Missing*, and "The Jeffersons." I chose the latter and turned the volume off, so I wouldn't miss a sound in the house.

I took two Sudafeds, made some hot milk, pulled on one of Avery's sweatshirts, and went to bed with the *Post-Gazette*. The front page was devoted to the search for Kevin Kogut. There was a picture of some cops and searchers pointing at the map tacked up in the gym at the school, and a picture of Marianne Dallas, swamped in a man's raincoat, crying. Underneath the picture it said, "Marianne Dallas, 35, pleads for information about whereabouts of her son Kevin, 14, and thanks volunteers for their efforts in the search."

The article didn't say anything about the library card or the picture of Avery. It did say that the chief of police "looked grim as he spoke to reporters. 'The longer the search goes on, the more worried we are,' he said."

I'll say, I thought, and pushed the newspaper down to the foot of the bed. The hot milk must have neutralized the Sudafeds; I felt relaxed for the first time in twenty-four hours. I gave Lucas another pat, fluffed up my pillow, and laid down my head.

I was almost asleep when the phone rang. Hoping it was Claire or Dan Sikora, I lunged across the bed to the bedside table, grabbed the receiver, and knocked the phone and the pile of magazines it was on to the floor.

"Hello," I said.

There was no response.

"Hello," I tried again.

I thought I could hear breathing, but maybe it was my own.

I was about to hang up, but then I heard a sound like a cough or somebody clearing his throat, and a child's voice came on the line.

"Is this Avery's sister?"

It was Kevin Kogut.

"Yes, this is Avery's sister. I'm Libby," I said.

He said nothing.

"Kevin," I said, "where are you?"

"I'm nowhere," he said. "I can't tell you."

"Is anybody with you?"

Again, nothing. I was afraid I was scaring him, afraid he would hang up.

"Kevin," I said, "I'm glad you called. Can I help you?"

He started to say something, but his voice was overwhelmed by the sound of traffic—a sound like a semi, or a couple of them, driving by fast. He must have been at a pay phone somewhere. Along some highway. Maybe at a truck stop.

Lucas got out of his dog bed and tried to get into the bed with me. I gave him a tug and a boost and he settled at my feet.

The sound of the truck passed.

Kevin came back on the line, and started talking—fast.

"I want you to take me to New York," he said. "I heard Mom and Ted talking when Avery died, and they said you lived in New York City."

"Of course I'll take you, Kevin," I said. "But how come?" I asked. "How come you want to go there?"

I worried that I was pressing my luck, asking too many questions. But he kept on talking.

"I think somebody killed Avery," he said. "I don't think he killed himself. I think somebody killed him."

He was starting to fall apart. His voice was breaking, and I didn't hear the last few words that he said.

"I'll come get you, Kevin," I said. "Don't worry," I said. "Tell me where you are and I'll come get you."

He stopped talking. But he didn't hang up. I prayed that he had enough dimes to keep the line alive.

He whispered now.

"I think somebody's trying to kill me too," he said.

I heard a car door slam and the sound of a couple of men shouting to each other.

"Who are those people, Kevin?" I asked. "Are those people that you know?"

"It's nobody," he said. "It's nobody I'm with. I'm just at a phone someplace."

"Where are you?" I said. "I need to know where you are so I can tell your mom and Ted that you're safe."

"Don't," he said. "Don't tell them anything."

He stopped talking again.

I was worried that I'd blown it—that he'd hang up.

"Kevin," I said, "what do you want me to do?"

A feminine computerized voice broke into the line.

"Please deposit sixty-five additional cents for five additional minutes," it said.

"I can't talk anymore," said Kevin.

"Kevin," I said, "I want to help you. I'll take you to New York. Just tell me where to come get you and when."

"I'll call you tomorrow morning," he said. "I'll call you at six o'clock tomorrow morning and tell you where to come."

"Okay, Kevin," I said. "Okay. I'll wait for your call."

I don't know if he heard me. The phone went dead.

I lay back down against the pillow and buried my feet under Lucas.

Kevin Kogut was alive. He was alive and somewhere nearby. He was somewhere a sixty-five-cent phone call away.

I picked up the phone and dialed directory information. The phone rang and rang, and then a man's voice came on the line. Even though I knew the answer, I asked him if there was any way of telling where a phone call I just received had come from.

"No," he said. "But we can make arrangements to change your phone number."

Then I asked him how far I could call on a sixty-five-cent, five-minute call from a pay phone.

"Not real far," he said. "Maybe Marshall, maybe Canton."

*   *   *

I lay in the bed and itched to call the police and Ted and Marianne, but the memory of the pleading sound in Kevin's voice held me back. I'll get him tomorrow, I thought. I'll get him, and I'll bring him home.

The house was very still. All I could hear was the murmur of the fish tank and Lucas's slow, deep snore.

Why would anyone want to kill a kid like Kevin Kogut?

I heard the rasp of tires on gravel and held my breath as headlights fanned past the house and a car headed down the road. Lucas moaned, kicked a leg, and lapsed again into his snoring sleep.

I got out of bed, put on the bathrobe that I'd put aside for Dan Sikora, and rifled through the kitchen drawers until I found a carving knife—a blunt old thing with a warped wooden handle. I sharpened it on a whetstone that I found on top of the refrigerator and brought it into the living room. I looked out the front window for a moment at the moon, hanging heavy and huge and lustrous against the cloudless, plum-black sky. I pulled the shades and, with shaking hands, laid the knife on the floor underneath the sofa. Then, with the overhead light still on, I turned facedown and fell asleep.

13

I was in a dead, dreamless sleep, but there were sounds. A hissing sound, like water running full blast in the shower—and a banging sound, like a screen door slamming shut over and over in the wind, and then another bang. And then I was awake and choking and I could barely see because of the black smoke that billowed through the room. Thick, gritty, confounding black smoke that filled the room like a blizzard and strangled my nose and my throat and my chest. I felt like I was drowning, but I couldn't be, because I was in Avery's living room.

A wash of orange spilled out of the bedroom and into the hall—spilled out and sucked back—and then I realized it was flames and the house was on fire, and Lucas staggered toward me from the hall. Staggered toward me impossibly slowly on his three legs—slowly and without making a sound, but with terrified eyes and with his fur in flames—the fur around his face and down the center of his back a mane of orange fire.

Part of my consciousness broke away and floated above me, and I watched myself take Avery's bathrobe from the couch, wad it up, plunge it into the aquarium, wrap it around Lucas, and steer him to the front door. And then I was yanking on the door handle with both arms, but the door wouldn't budge, so I lifted up the coffee table and drove it through the front window and tried to smash the broken glass that clung to the edges of the window frame with a book that had been on the table. There was an intense, unbearable blast of heat. I shoved Lucas through the window with all my strength and leapt out after him.

People ran toward me from the road—a woman in a fringed white leather jacket and a man in a red parka. Then another man and a woman came running through the orchard next to Avery's house, and I told everyone that no, no one else was inside. Then someone gave me a man's overcoat to wrap myself in, and we stood in a little group on the lawn in front of the house and watched the flames leaking out of the bedroom windows and then out of the living room window, and watched the black smoke turn purple as it rose against the moon and plumed and coiled and rose again and finally disappeared. I wanted to take a picture and then I chided myself for being so perverse and I tried to remember where I'd put my camera the night before and realized I had no idea at all.

Fire engines came and a fireman asked me if anybody was inside, and again I said no. Then one of them asked me where I kept the keys to the truck and must have found them on the hook inside the front door, because I saw somebody back the truck out of the driveway and park it in the road. Somebody else made us stand in the field across the road, and then the couple who had come through the orchard brought Lucas and me to their house.

She was tall, gray-haired, and around fifty. Her name was Becky Bullock, and she was very worried about me and Lucas, but especially about Lucas, who was wheezing and singed and sorry-looking. I splashed cold water on my face and my arms in the kitchen sink while she called her brother, a doctor, who said he'd be right over. My eyes burned the way they do after too long a day at the beach, and I could feel a gash on my upper lip. A long, thin cut arced from the base of my right thumb to the inside of my elbow. The blood had clotted, and I marveled at how the wound had taken a path that barely avoided the intersection of veins just below the surface on the inside of my wrist. I wondered if there were any slivers of glass left inside.

I sat at the kitchen table and drank the orange juice that the woman poured for me out of a little white jug, ate a poached egg, looked out the big picture window at the orchard, and realized with surprise that it was growing light outside. The clock on the stove said 6:55. I dropped my head into my hands.

"Damn it," I said.

Becky came over and put her hand on my shoulder.

"There, there, dear," she said. "It's a setback, I know, but you're still alive."

I ran out the door and through the orchard to Avery's. I grabbed the first fireman I could.

"Did you hear a phone ringing in there? Did you hear a phone ringing about an hour ago?"

He shook me off his arm and reached down to the driveway to lift up a section of hose.

"Lady," he said, "we got this call at four o'clock. There's no way these telephones still work."

It couldn't be. I ran toward the house to find out for myself. Maybe Kevin would be late—maybe I had the time wrong—but another man in a black-and-yellow coat grabbed me by the arm and steered me back down the driveway.

"There's nothing you can save in there now," he said. "It's either burned or soaked or too hot to touch."

I sat down on the ground by the pine trees at the end of the driveway and burst into tears of frustration. This was impossible. Kevin was counting on me. Maybe he was trying to call right now—trying to call but the call wouldn't go through because the lines had burned. And what would he get? A busy signal? A message from the operator telling him that sorry, this number was no longer in service? What should I do now? Call the cops and Ted and Marianne and tell them that I'd found Kevin but that I'd lost him again?

Lucas was howling—a rasping, sad howl that carried from the neighbors' house and through the orchard. I walked back through the apple trees and into the Bullocks' kitchen. A man with red hair and thick eyeglasses said he was Becky's brother and could he take a look at my arms, which he did, and could he take a listen to my chest, which he also did. And then he poked into the cut on my arm with a pair of long, thin tweezers and pulled out a little chunk of glass and then another, smaller one, and rubbed some ointment on the burned part of my forearms, chin, nose, and forehead, and said it could have been much worse—it could have been far, far worse.

I thanked him and rubbed at the face of my watch with a paper napkin. The smoke had discolored it, and the broken glass had ripped the surface of the leather band, but it was still ticking.

I hugged Lucas and tried to get him to drink some water, which he wouldn't do, and then I went to the bathroom and looked in the mirror and saw that I had no eyebrows, just the ridges where they used to be, and that my widow's peak had burned off too, and that the gash on my lip felt much worse than it looked.

I sat on the edge of the tub and gave myself a sort of sitz bath, trying not to wash off the salve on my arms, and then I put on the corduroy pants and flannel shirt that Becky Bullock had put out for me, laced up a pair of her old running shoes, which were a remarkably good fit, and swallowed three aspirin from a bottle that I found in the medicine chest.

A fireman and a cop were in the kitchen when I came out of the bathroom. The cop was Duane—the guy with the mangy sideburns who'd answered my call the night before. He was tilting way back in Becky Bullock's chrome and marbleized-yellow-vinyl dinette chair, with his legs spread apart, and he didn't look very happy. I noticed that he had thick black hair on the backs of his hands and wondered if he had it on his back too.

I poured another cup of Becky Bullock's coffee and guzzled half of it.

"Did you make your call to the insurance company yet?" he asked.

I thought he was talking to the fireman.

He swung forward in the chair and slammed his feet down.

"I'm talking to you, Miss Smartmouth," he said. "How much do you have the place covered for?"

I was still missing the point.

"Okay," he said, "what's the name of the insurance company?"

It dawned on me that he thought I knew who Avery's insurer was. Maybe he was going to call them to come out and look at the rubble.

"You inherited the place from your brother, didn't you?" he said. "So how much insurance did he take out on it? Or are you going to try to tell me that you don't know?"

The black coffee cleared my head. It dawned on me that this cretin was suggesting that I had burned Avery's house down to make money. What was wrong with this guy? Why was he so suspicious of me? Did he hate women? Just women from New York? Just me?

"Wait a minute," I said. "I just came damn near close to getting killed in there—and you're trying to tell me that I started the fire myself?"

Duane smirked. "That's what you're saying," he said, "not me."

I resisted the impulse to throw my coffee mug at him and set it down on the table instead.

"Officer," I said, "I think you're really out of line. I don't know much about the law, but I do know that there's such a thing as defamation, and I think you're the one who's playing with fire here—not me."

The fireman, who had been writing things down on a clipboard, intervened.

"Cut it out, Duane," he said. "She's right. You're acting out of line here. In fact, I don't know that we need you in on this conversation in the first place. I think the guys can use some help with the hoses."

Duane refused to get the message, folded his arms across his chest, and scowled at the two of us.

The fireman continued. "I'm Dave Thellman. What do you think started the fire? Did you have a space heater going?"

"No."

"Stove on?"

I tried to replay the hours before I'd gone to sleep. I'd made some hot milk, but surely . . .

"I made some hot milk," I said.

Duane made a sound like a choked laugh and rolled his eyes.

Dave Thellman wrote furiously on his notepad.

When had Kevin called? Ten-thirty? Ten-forty? I'd drunk the milk just before he called. Hadn't I turned off the stove and set the pan to soak in the sink?

"But I must have turned the stove off," I said. "I must have put the pan in the sink to soak."

"Suzy Homemaker," said Duane.

"Shut up," said Thellman.

"Are you a smoker?" said Thellman. "Was anybody smoking in there last night?"

"Smoking what?" said Duane. "That's what I'd like to know."

Thellman slammed the clipboard down. At the same moment the back door opened and two more firemen came in, their faces gray with soot and strain. They yanked off their boots and hats and joined us in the kitchen.

One of them was completely bald. He identified himself to me as somebody Jenkins, the fire chief, and the others, even Duane, were suitably deferential.

He seemed to know Becky Bullock, and they talked for a few minutes about Becky's son, who, it turned out, played basketball for Ohio State. She plucked two poached eggs from the pan and put them in front of Jenkins at the table.

When he turned to me, he was all business.

"Miss Kincaid," he said, "we have reason to believe that this fire was deliberately set."

Duane smirked.

"Why?" I asked.

"From the pattern of the flames," he said, "which started along the outside of the house by the bedroom, and from traces of gasoline on the foundation on that side of the house. It looks like someone tried to burn you in your bedroom."

My shoulders and head gave an involuntary shudder.

"Did you hear anybody?" he said.

"No," I said. "But I was sleeping hard. I'd just taken some cold medication, and I was exhausted. I was sleeping on the sofa in the living room because I was a nervous wreck from hearing somebody prowl around the house the night before."

Jenkins's eyes lit up. "A prowler?"

"Yes. A prowler. Duane here could tell you all about it. I called the police on Wednesday night because I heard somebody walking on the driveway and I saw somebody disappear into the trees down at the end of the driveway."

"We checked it out, Chief," said Duane. "It was nothing. Just her imagination."

Jenkins ignored him.

"Miss Kincaid," he said, "we're bringing in the police department for a full arson investigation. In fact, the investigators may be here now. Where can we reach you if we need to talk with you?"

Good question. I thought about giving him Sikora's number but didn't. Somehow I didn't want to subject Dan to Duane's malicious scrutiny. Besides, I needed a place to call my own right now, and who knew when Sikora would get back?

"At the Arrowhead Motel," I said. "You know, the place out on Route 6."

"By the Rollercade," said Jenkins.

"By the Rollercade," I said.

"And, Miss Kincaid," said Jenkins.

"Yes?"

"Have you called your insurer yet?"

"I don't even know who my insurer is," I said. "If I've got any information about that, it was with a pile of papers that Avery's lawyer gave me about the estate, and they've probably burned up along with the bedroom."

"You'd better talk with Avery's lawyer," he said.

"Yeah," chimed in Duane. "You better get a lawyer."

Then they left. Just like that. No more questions about who the prowler was or who could the prowler be or did I have any thoughts as to why someone would try to set fire to the house I was sleeping in. They stuffed themselves back into their slickers and plodded back through the orchard to Avery's.

I sat with Becky Bullock for a while at the table, drinking more orange juice, and assured her that I would take Lucas to the vet's as soon as I could. I called Doug Pope's office, and the man who answered the phone said Pope wasn't in yet and told me to call back later.

I accepted Becky Bullock's offer of a long-term loan of a sweater and another flannel shirt and a wool baseball jacket, and headed back to Avery's with Lucas.

Whoever had found the keys to Avery's truck had left them in the ignition. I boosted Lucas into the cab with me and rejoiced when I spied a lump under the blanket on the floor. It was my camera. For the first time in my life I'd been dumb enough to forget to bring it in with me at night, and it was exactly the right night to do it. I took it out of the camera bag and held it in my hand for a moment, comforted by its familiar weight and by the feel of the smooth metal casing. A folded envelope protruded from the pocket in the back of the bag. It was the money that Sikora had paid me for Avery's investment in the Vroman pictures. I had forgotten to put it in my wallet, which was in the pocket of my jacket, which was no doubt incinerated in Avery's bedroom. I had a little luck left after all.

14

The Arrowhead Motel parking lot was empty except for a rusted-out powder-blue Mustang with a bumper sticker in the back window that said I AM THE MAN YOUR MOTHER WARNED YOU ABOUT. I parked at the far end of the lot, out of view, I hoped, from the check-in area, and told Lucas to stay quiet while I was gone.

I needn't have worried that anyone in the office was watching Lucas and me in the truck. The only person there was the woman with the cookie-jar hairdo and exotic finger-nails, who was transfixed by a rerun of "The Love Boat." I asked her for a room at the far end of the building, claiming that I thought it would be quietest there, but really in an effort to keep Lucas out of sight. She took my cash and handed me my room key wordlessly, her eyes bolted to the screen. I noticed that there was something odd about her propor-tions—not just that she had a giant hairdo but that her neck seemed large for her body, and so did her hands.

Good God, I thought. Is this woman THE MAN YOUR MOTHER WARNED YOU ABOUT? I shuddered, nipped the thought in the bud, and headed for my room.

The room was a replica of the one I'd been in before, ex-cept the chintzy floral polyester bedspread was a symphony of green and pink instead of a symphony of yellow and orange. The gold-colored shag carpeting was the same, though, and I wondered if the health code didn't require motel owners to peel it off the floor and install something fresh, say, once every twenty years or so.

Lucas was in dog heaven. The place reeked—human smells, antiseptic smells, room deodorizer smells, and smells in the carpet from the thousand other dogs and cats that people had sneaked in for the night. He rooted around the drapes and the hem of the bedspread like a pig going for truffles. I cranked open the window, lay down on the bed, and breathed in the breeze. Better than living in the truck, I thought.

I called Pam Bates's number. An answering service replied, and a woman asked me if it was an emergency. Lucas still looked like a bedraggled, charbroiled mess, but was at that very moment trying to drink from the toilet bowl. I said no, it wasn't an emergency. She told me that Pam would be in the clinic at ten, and I left the message that Lucas and I would be there then.

I tried Dan Sikora's number. Still no answer. Had he told me when he was coming back? Did I imagine that he said he'd be back today? I couldn't get Kevin Kogut out of my mind. I could hear his voice, thin and plaintive, in my ear.

"I'll call you tomorrow morning," he'd said. "I'll call you at six o'clock tomorrow morning and tell you where to come."

I called the Dallases. I could tell them that Kevin had called me and the line had gone dead. They'd be angry that I hadn't called them earlier, but at least they'd know that he was alive.

I let it ring twenty times, but there was no answer. I couldn't call the cops. That Duane fellow had me pegged for a criminal myself. They'd put me in jail for obstruction of justice or something.

I called Doug Pope again, and this time he answered the phone himself.

"Fire?" he said. "That's too bad. That's really too bad."

He took a long time to get the file.

"The insurers," he said. "The insurers. Oh, yes, here we go: Avery's policy was with Three Rivers Mutual. Try Hank Clark at Three Rivers and tell him Doug sent you."

I tried Hank Clark, who asked for directions to Avery's house and said he'd meet me there at noon to help me submit my claim. I was flabbergasted. The only experience I'd ever had with insurance companies had been the eternal process of trying to collect for a bent fender.

The Arrowhead was extremely quiet. The only sounds I could hear were the hum of a vacuum cleaner a couple of rooms away and the occasional passing car. I looked at the door and its flimsy nickel-plated lock. In fact, it wasn't really a lock at all—just a doorknob with a button in the center.

I wondered if I'd made a mistake by asking for a room this far from the office. I wondered if I'd made a mistake coming to the Arrowhead at all. Plenty of people knew that I'd stayed here when I first came to town. And there was Avery's truck, right outside the room. I might as well have asked the check-in lady to spell "Welcome Libby Kincaid to Room 8A" on the sign in front of the building.

Somebody pounded on the door, and I sat upright on the bed. I could see through the window that it was a seventeen-year-old kid, dragging a vacuum cleaner as big as a Maytag washer.

I opened the door, and he stepped into the room, tugging the vacuum behind him. Lucas limped out of the bathroom, and the boy stared at him as though he were a boa constrictor.

"No pets allowed in the rooms," he said. "Manager's orders."

I wanted to clobber the guy, but then I realized what a nightmare Lucas looked like. The three legs were odd enough, but combined with his frizzled, blackened, burned-off fur, the effect was alarming.

"Manager's orders," said the kid, his eyes glued to Lucas. "They stink up the place."

I tried to appeal to his softer side.

"Look," I said. "He's sick. Just a sick old dog, and I have to take care of him."

He was backing away now. I suppose he thought whatever Lucas had was infectious.

He was standing out on the sidewalk.

"I'm going to have to call the management," he said. "We can't have no sick dogs here."

I thought about driving up to Salem and checking into the Econo Lodge I'd seen there. I thought about driving back to Becky Bullock's and asking her for refuge for the night. I thought about getting in the truck right then and there and driving straight to New York.

"Okay," I said. "I'll take the dog someplace else. But give me a few minutes, all right?"

I was at Pam Bates's clinic inside half an hour. She was standing in the back entrance to the reception area, giving instructions to a teenage girl in a lab coat about what to do with a white cat lying listlessly on a table. Pam looked up briefly as Lucas and I walked in—not registering that we were there at first—then swung her head back to us with a look of horror on her face.

"What happened?"

She was all over Lucas, looking at his stump wound, looking in his eyes, feeling his stomach.

"What happened?" she said. "What did you do to him?"

The parrot in the cage next to the reception desk began to shriek and thump around, and a dog, or maybe a couple of them, began howling in one of the back rooms. The girl in the lab coat pulled a sheet over the birdcage, and the din subsided.

"I didn't do anything to him," I said. "Avery's house burned down last night, and Lucas and I were inside."

She looked at me blankly, as if I had just told her that there were two blue cars in her parking lot, or something equally unamazing.

"Avery's house burned down," she said, quietly and without inflection. And again, "Avery's house burned down."

She steered Lucas into the examining room, and I helped her to lift him to the table.

She took a flashlight and looked down his throat and in his ears, and into his eyes again. Then she examined every inch of him—the pads of his feet, his back, his belly, his nose, his tail—without saying a word to me, but cooing all the while at Lucas. Lucas didn't resist for a moment; he lay there wearily, resignedly, occasionally looking into my face or into Pam's with his huge brown eyes for reassurance.

She poured water from the faucet into a big aluminum dog dish and put it in front of him. Lucas lapped up a little, then guzzled the rest of the bowl.

Pam acknowledged me for the first time since the examination began.

"He's okay," she said. "He looks a lot worse than he feels."

I felt my knees begin to buckle beneath me, and my hands and face went clammy with cold sweat. I groped my way to the chair next to the door.

"And I feel a lot worse than I look," I said.

I sat down and dunked my head between my knees.

Pam Bates ripped a little paper packet from where it had been taped to the wall, tore it open, and passed it back and forth beneath my nostrils. It was smelling salts or something, and the fumes jolted me back to consciousness so fast I should have gotten whiplash.

Pam gave me a glass of water and asked me if I wanted to lie down on the table. I wanted to lie down, but on a sofa somewhere, not on a dog-examining table. I told her I'd rather just sit still for a few minutes.

She leaned against the table, put her hands in her lab-coat pockets, and looked at me. For a moment I thought that she was about to say something kind or reassuring. Maybe she was, but then she changed her mind.

"How in the hell," she said, "did Avery's house burn down?"

And then, "Forget it. You're in no condition to talk. I can read it in the paper."

She let her eyes rove over my body, from singed bangs to battered arms to Becky Bullock's frayed running shoes.

"You and Darby don't seem like a good mix. If I were you, I'd go back to New York."

"Thanks for the hospitality, Pam," I said.

"I'm not trying to be mean," she said. "But you Kincaids seem to be on a losing streak this year, Lucas included. Get out now. I'm serious."

She beckoned to her assistant to help her get Lucas off the table, patted Lucas on the neck, and left the room.

Lucas ambled over to me and leaned against my leg. I sat still awhile longer to make sure that my fainting spell, or whatever it was, was over, then got up to leave.

The assistant was writing on a chart. When she was finished, I explained that I had to stay in a motel and asked her if there was any room in the kennel for Lucas tonight, and maybe for tomorrow night too.

She told me that I was in luck—someone had just canceled some vacation plans—and motioned me to bring Lucas out back. I gave Lucas a rub behind the ears and a nuzzle on the neck, and promised that I'd be back real soon. Then I got the blanket from Avery's car and dropped it over the pen door next to Lucas. I could hear him whimpering as I walked back into the building with the assistant, and I couldn't let myself look back at him for fear I'd burst into tears.

I could see Pam in the second examining room, talking with a man and a young boy about a German shepherd puppy that was running around in circles at the boy's feet. She looked up at me as I walked by. I told her that Lucas was in the kennel, and said thanks and goodbye, but Pam said nothing. She had either miraculous powers of concentration or an endless capacity for rudeness.

*   *   *

I drove straight to Avery's for my twelve o'clock appointment with Hank Clark, but he beat me to it. By the time I
arrived he'd already talked with the arson investigator and
taken his own photographs.

He was grinning from ear to ear. I wondered if he thought
claims verification was really fun, or if the smile was just a
nervous habit.

I sat with him in his car, a big beige Buick with automatic
everything, which he'd parked in the street, and he gave me
a form on a clipboard to fill out, which I did.

He gave me another big smile and said, "This could take
a little longer than the usual to process, Miss Kincaid. Not
that I think the office will have a problem with it. But the
officers over there think there was arson involved. Did you
know that, Miss Kincaid?"

"Yes," I said. "I know that."

"Is that the kind of thing kids do around here?" he asked.

"I don't know," I said. "I'm not from around here."

"That's right," he said. "That's what the officers said. So
I'm sure you understand," he continued, "that in circum-
stances like these we have to conduct our own investigation.
Purely a formality. I'm sure you understand."

"Of course," I said. "I understand."

I got out of the car. Hank Clark pushed a couple of buttons, and all the windows rolled up and all the doors locked
at the same time. I waved goodbye as he backed out the drive,
but I don't think he noticed.

There were only two people at Avery's now. As I stood in
the driveway I could see them: Chief Jenkins, whom I had
talked with in the morning, and a small black woman dressed
in a bright-green jogging outfit. They were walking along the
outside of the house where Avery's bedroom was, measuring

a distance on the ground by the foundation with a yellow measuring tape.

I walked toward them and they ignored me. The woman, like every other public servant I'd seen in Marshall County, had a clipboard, tucked into the crook of her arm. Jenkins yelled out some numbers to her, and she wrote them down. Then she yelled out some numbers to Jenkins, and he wrote them down on his clipboard.

I introduced myself to the woman, who, after glancing up to Jenkins, introduced herself to me.

"I'm Jeanette Nelson," she said. "Sergeant Nelson."

Jenkins interrupted.

"Nelson, here," he said, "she's our arson expert. She says she wants to ask you a few questions."

Can firemen arrest you? I wondered if I needed a lawyer.

"Relax," she said. "I just need to know some things about what you heard and saw and where you heard and saw it." She stood with the exaggerated good posture of a dancer— shoulders back, toes turned out—and she spoke in clipped, precise tones.

I went through everything I'd already covered with Jenkins in the morning. No, I didn't smoke. No, I didn't hear anybody outside. I was sleeping in the living room because I didn't feel like sleeping in the bedroom. No, I didn't smell anything funny before I realized the place was on fire.

Jeanette Nelson glanced up from her clipboard and looked me steadily in the face.

"Miss Kincaid," she said, "it looks to me like somebody tried to kill you last night. Somebody ran a crowbar through the door handle on the front door and a broomstick through the handle on the back door so you couldn't get out, and somebody poured some accelerant—maybe kerosene, maybe gasoline, we don't know yet—along the outside of the house where your bedroom was. Do you have any idea who would want to do a thing like that to you?"

That explained why I'd tugged and tugged on the front

door and nothing had happened. How long had I stood there, my heart frozen in terror, pulling with all my strength? My hands got clammy as the scene replayed in my mind.

"Miss Kincaid," she said, "why did we find a knife under the sofa that you say you were sleeping on? Who is it that you're so afraid of?"

What could I say? Of course somebody was after me. But her guess was as good as mine.

"You're right," I said. "And I'm sure you know as well as I do that I called the police the night before last because I heard somebody—no, I saw somebody—prowling around the house, but they didn't take it very seriously."

At least she didn't think I burned the place down myself, like Duane did. A minor load off my mind.

"We've had a report," she said, "that you may be involved in some drug trafficking."

"What!" I felt like somebody socked me. "What kind of report? Who said that to you?"

But I didn't need to ask. I knew it had to be Duane. I remembered the comments he'd made to me about my red eyes when he'd come to the house. The guy was a lunatic. What had he done? Seen my cold medicine on the side of the sink and written me off as a junkie?

"Forget it," she said. "I shouldn't have said anything."

Shrewd operator, I thought. She says something outrageous to see what kind of reaction she gets out of me, and then she pretends it was a slip of the tongue. Wasn't she violating my constitutional rights or something? I hadn't watched enough "L.A. Law" to know.

I felt a hand on my shoulder and spun around.

It was Dan Sikora.

"Hey," he said. "What's going on?" He was glancing back and forth between me and the carcass of Avery's house, a look of horror on his face.

I explained to him the obvious—that Avery's house had caught fire last night—and then the not so obvious: that it hadn't been an accident, and that it looked like somebody tried to trap Lucas and me in the inferno.

"Lucas?" he said. "Is he—"

"Thank God, no," I said. "He's at Pam Bates's, because I'm back at the Arrowhead."

Jenkins and Jeanette Nelson appeared to be packing up to leave. I asked them if I could go inside—if the floor would collapse or if the walls would cave in.

Jenkins told me that it was safe to go back, and Nelson agreed.

"In fact," she said, "if I were you, I'd salvage as much of your brother's things now as I could. We're supposed to be in for rain tonight, and this place isn't as watertight as it used to be."

And how. Somebody had nailed some flimsy sheets of plywood over the broken windows, and there was a hole in Avery's bedroom wall so big you could use it for a door.

The chief and Jeanette Nelson walked on out to Jenkins's car. I heard the engine start up as Sikora and I walked through the place where the front door used to be.

The fire department had apparently come before the flames devoured the living room. The wall nearest the hall was scorched, especially around the fish tank. Nothing else seemed to have burned, but the scene was grim. The room looked like a trendy Manhattan discotheque; the walls and ceiling were black with smoke, remnants of drapes hung in twisted hunks from the broken, boarded-up windows, and the rug was gray and soggy beneath our feet.

I didn't need to touch the books in the bookcase to know that they had been ruined. The pages were bloated with water; the bindings had split from the strain. Avery's once-immaculate magazine collection was a congealed lump in a puddle on the floor.

The fish tank stood askew on its stand, partially full of water. I didn't look inside. Whatever I hadn't killed when I'd stuffed Avery's bathrobe inside the tank was surely dead by now.

I sat down on the sofa, sank into a cold, sodden, spongy mass, and jumped right up again. I started to laugh—a touch of hysteria, I suppose—and Sikora joined in. But I noticed that his eyes were full of tears, and his voice was husky when he spoke.

"It was all that was left," he said. "It was all that was left of Avery, and now it's gone too."

He wiped the glass of the framed poster over the mantel with the back of his hand, revealing part of the humpback whale in the picture. Then he lifted up Avery's Indian pot, which, through some fluke, remained intact on the mantel.

"Here," he said. "You'll want to put this somewhere safe."

I held it, and we continued our tour of the damage.

Avery's bedroom was a complete loss. The flames had burned the wallpaper off the walls and the rug off the floor. The bed frame, which must have been made of a hard wood that took a long time to combust, was blackened but in one piece. The blankets, sheets, and most of the mattress had burned away, and I shuddered to think that I had lain there only a few hours before the fire had hit. The tidy piles of Avery's clothes that I had made the night before had simply disappeared. So had most of the cheap wooden bureau that stood in the corner. The computer terminal was blackened and deformed. I wondered what had happened to the glass that had been the screen; it seemed to have evaporated.

As we stood there, I told Sikora about the prowler I had seen on Wednesday night, and about how, because of an inexplicable hunch, or the happy hand of fate, I had slept last night on the sofa instead of the bed. I told him about the way Lucas had looked, staggering into the living room, his fur in flames. I told him about the phone call from Kevin Kogut, and about Duane's suggestion that I had burned the place down myself. I surprised myself with the calmness with which I recounted a tale that sounded, even to me, like something dreamed up to cram action into a half-hour television show.

Sikora never said a word, but stood there with a look of mixed incredulity and concern on his face.

"You sure know how to shake a place up," he said.

"I didn't exactly do it to get your attention."

"Thanks," he said. And then, "You're not staying at any motel tonight. I think you'd better stay with me."

It sounded a little too John Wayneish for my taste, but I was too tired to resist.

The electricity was out in the house, so we decided to do what we could with Avery's things before the sun went down. Sikora drove to the U-Haul rental place to get some cardboard boxes, and I wandered through the rest of the rooms.

Portions of the hallway were charred, and the remaining wallpaper had buckled from the water, but I supposed that the space could be restored with some effort. The kitchen, like everything else in the house, was coated with ash and soot.

I groped my way down the basement stairs and felt for the flashlight that I remembered having seen hanging from the pegboard over Avery's workbench. I shone it across the basement. The only damage seemed to be a leak from the water on the living room floor. I found a bucket, positioned it under the leak, and listened to the strident pinging as I climbed back up the stairs.

Sikora and I assembled the boxes and filled them quickly, silently, and methodically, like people working in a sweatshop. Without the items from his bedroom, and without the books, which we decided were past saving, Avery owned very little. I grew sadder as I remembered the small treasures, all of them destroyed by the fire, that I had placed in the box on Avery's bureau the night before—especially the picture of my mother.

We finished the living room in forty-five minutes and packed up the kitchen in an hour. We took Avery's fishing rods from the basement and decided to pack up the rest of his tackle when we could arrange for better light.

The skies darkened as we loaded the boxes into the back of the pickup. Sikora decided that Avery's mission chairs could recover with some care, and wedged them on top of the boxes. We stretched a tarp that I found in the basement across the top of the pile, and then Dan got into his van. I drove behind him, Avery's Indian pot nestled in my lap.

I felt like a wartime refugee, or a fugitive.

15

The skies broke open as we pulled onto the scrap of pavement behind Sikora's store. We unloaded the truck as quickly as we could, the cardboard boxes dissolving in our hands, and threaded our way through the junk Sikora kept behind the building—cast-off radiators, pedestal sinks, a wooden sign from an amusement park that said TUNNEL OF LOVE—and down a decrepit flight of wooden stairs into the basement. We stuffed the boxes into what available space we could find— underneath a mammoth soapstone sink and behind a furnace that looked like Rube Goldberg built it—and left Avery's chairs outside, wrapped in the tarp.

It was dark as we climbed the stairs to Sikora's apartment. I was shivering, soaked to the skin, and could think of nothing but sleep. Sikora heated up some soup on the stove while I ran water for a bath, and then he found me some sweatpants and a sweatshirt to change into. They were obviously a woman's size, but I decided to be circumspect for once and didn't ask any questions. I squeezed what dampness I could out of the clothes Becky Bullock had loaned me and hung them over the radiator to dry, or fry, as the case might be.

I lowered myself into the tub and went about the delicate

task of trying to bathe myself without getting the burns on my arms wet.

The bathroom door, coated with twelve or so layers of paint, wouldn't close all the way, and Sikora took advantage of the problem by keeping up a conversation while I was in the tub.

"You need a rest," he said.

"You bet."

"Maybe you ought to go home for a few days and recuperate."

"Thanks a lot. What are you, anyway, the Anti-Welcome Wagon?"

"I'm serious," he said. "I think it's time for you to call it quits."

I yanked on the sweatclothes. I was furious.

"Look," I said to him, "you're supposed to be on my side. You're supposed to be sticking this out with me because of Avery."

He didn't respond.

I felt we were reenacting the scene in Sikora's shop from the week before, when I'd tried to talk with him about Avery and he'd been so remote.

I sat down at the card table that he'd set for dinner and waited for him to talk.

He poured the soup from the saucepan into two old, shallow china bowls. Then he sawed some bread off a loaf, buttered a piece for him and a piece for me, and set them on the table. I could tell from his face that he wasn't avoiding answering me; he was trying to think of what to say.

I ate the soup and swabbed out the bowl with the bread. In the bottom of the bowl there was a blurry, cracked pink-and-white picture of a man pushing a woman in a swing that hung from a willow tree on the edge of a river. The man had a creepy little grin on his face, and I wondered for a moment if he planned to knock his true love off her perch and into the river.

Sikora watched me eat.

"Libby," he said, "I know you'll think that this sounds old-fashioned, or maybe you'll think that I'm abandoning you somehow, but the truth is that I'm worried about you. Worried that someone is going to kill you. I think you ought to get out of Darby."

"Thanks," I said.

"Maybe you're safer when you're with me," he said, "but maybe you're not. I don't think that whoever set Avery's house on fire with you inside would have cared if I'd been in there, too, and if I had, I might not have been able to prevent what happened."

I felt too tired—too defeated maybe—to argue. And a part of me agreed with him. I was scared. As scared as I'd ever been since I was a kid being shipped off to live with relatives I'd hardly ever heard of in New York State. But I could barely admit that to myself, much less to Sikora. If I ever admitted to myself that I was scared, how could I get anything done? How could I live in Manhattan? How could I take pictures? How could I make peace with Avery?

By the time I surfaced from my reverie, Sikora had done the dishes and was brewing tea in an old brown pot with a chip in the lid.

"So stay here as long as you want," he said.

He pulled a record out of an album sleeve and laid it on a turntable that was on top of a wooden file cabinet.

"I want to help you," he said. "But I don't know how. All I can think to tell you is to lay low. To stay out of sight until something happens that makes it clear what the right next step is."

"Like what?" I asked. "An angel who visits me in a dream?"

This was all I needed—for Dan Sikora to go mystical on me in my hour of need.

The voice of Patsy Cline streamed, smoky and sweet, from the speaker.

Crazy,
Crazy for feelin' so lonely;

I'm crazy,
Crazy for feelin' so blue.

"Maybe not an angel," he said. And then, "Libby, I know it might seem to you like I don't know anything but old pictures, but I've had some experiences in my life that make me convinced that you shouldn't do anything without having a reason for doing it. Do you understand what I'm saying?"

"Not really," I said.

And I didn't. In photography, I work on instinct. Feel the picture first, push the shutter, and think later.

"Maybe you will after you sleep on it," he said.

He knelt down next to the sofa, reached underneath, pulled out a large black portfolio case, and brought it over to the table.

"Your mind needs some diversion," he said. "Take a look at these."

I took the portfolio to the couch and laid it open next to me. There were eight copy prints of the Adam Clark Vroman photographs that Sikora and Avery had invested in. I recognized the pictures immediately because I'd seen them endless times in books and journals.

"Bart's got the originals," said Sikora, "in his vault."

"You hope," I almost said. But I didn't.

The first was a portrait of a group of Hopi women and girls, some of them with their hair arranged in fantastical, glistening buns that extended high and outward above their ears, like Princess Leia in *Star Wars;* the next was a portrait of a young Hopi woman seated in a doorway, nursing her child. There was a portrait of a man weaving a blanket, and another of a woman making a basket. There were two portraits of Nampeyo, the famous Hopi potter. In one she crouched on the ground, kneading clay; in the other she was firing pots in an outdoor kiln made from rocks. Then there was a portrait of a group of men, two of whom were examining sheets of paper so intensely that they didn't look up for the camera. I remembered reading somewhere that they were looking at pictures that Vroman had taken on a previous trip.

The next print was a portrait of a young Hopi woman wearing the traditional hairdress, staring fully and placidly at the camera with enormous dark eyes, her neck rimmed with heavy silver jewelry, her face and eyelashes dusted with a fine, light powder.

The fact that these were copy prints did little to lessen the impact of the pictures. They were marvels of composition—tributes, you could say, to the intimate relationship that Vroman had with his subjects. Looking into the faces in these portraits was like gazing into the eyes of people you've known all your life—people you would trust with your deepest secrets.

I stacked the pictures neatly and looked up at Sikora.

He was smiling. Not a great big grin or anything—but he was smiling, and he looked relaxed and pleased and proud, like a parent showing off photographs of his newborn. I thought that maybe this was the first time I had ever seen him look happy.

The last two prints in the pile were separated from the others by a thin sheet of paper and were slightly larger than the rest. Sikora watched me lift them from the pile.

"These are the real treasures," he said. "These are the prints we made from the glass plates that came with the purchase. Bart did the printing. They could be a lot better, but it gives you the idea."

I took the prints to the kitchen table, where the light was slightly better, and laid them down, side by side.

They were portraits of two young Hopi men.

"Nobody knows about them," said Sikora. "No curators, no historians, no collectors—not even the Vroman family, as far as we can tell."

One picture was of a man wearing large, slender silver hoop earrings and a dark, broad-brimmed felt hat decorated with a white ribbon. His face was young, his features were delicate. He was sitting cross-legged on the ground on a striped blanket, and he was holding a hammer so small it looked almost like a toy. Spread on the blanket before him, in a semicircle, were sheets of what appeared to be silver, something that looked like a small vise, and several pieces of silver jewelry.

The tonalities of the print were lovely, and typically Vroman. Even in this print, which, as Sikora said, wasn't the best quality, the white band on the man's hat gleamed with a soft luminescence—as though it were lit from behind—and the skin of the man's face shone like something that had been burnished by hand.

The second was a head-and-shoulders portrait of a broad-faced man with a dark-colored scarf wrapped around his forehead and knotted over one ear, posed against an adobe wall. He, too, was wearing large hoop earrings, but these were threaded with silver beads. The man's eyes were closed, and his cheeks and nose were smeared with a light-colored paint that shone as though it were metallic. The man's face was tranquil—beatific, even. I wondered if he had been sharing a little weed with the photographer from the city.

And I wondered if Vroman had discarded the plate because the man's eyes were closed. If he had, it was a mistake. The picture was extraordinary in every way. I agreed with Sikora: The two portraits ranked with the most beautiful of Vroman's photographs.

I certainly had never seen the portraits before—not in any book or exhibition catalog. How could they have eluded the Vroman experts for so long?

"How can you know, Dan," I asked, "how can you know for certain that they're Vromans—that nobody's pulling a hoax on you?"

Sikora retrieved the pile of copy prints from the sofa and separated the group portrait of the Hopi men from the others. He laid it on the table with the two Vroman treasures.

It took me only a moment to realize that the glass plates were absolutely, unequivocally Vroman's. The portraits

printed from the glass plates were individual portraits of two
of the men who had posed for the group portrait, and Vroman had clearly taken them a short time before or after he
had taken the group photograph. Their clothes, their jewelry, and their faces were exactly the same.

Sikora watched me as I made the discovery. He was still
smiling, and now he looked smug too.

"You're right," I said. "You've stumbled on buried treasure."

"It belongs to Avery too," he said.

Sikora took the portfolio and put it back where he had
gotten it. I lay down on the sofa and drifted off while Patsy
swung into her final number.

16

I woke up in the dark, and panicked for a moment when I realized that I wasn't at home, wasn't at Avery's, wasn't at the Arrowhead. As my eyes adjusted to the darkness, I realized where I was, and that the sounds that had awakened me were the sounds of Sikora in the bathroom, running the faucet and brushing his teeth. My watch said four-thirty.

I was still on the sofa. It was too short for sleeping, and my knees, which I'd tucked up to one side while I slept, ached. But I had a pillow under my head and a quilt wrapped around the rest of me, courtesy of Dan, I guessed.

The kettle started whistling softly on the stove. Sikora darted out of the bathroom, snatched it off the burner, and disappeared back into the bathroom.

I was impressed. I'd never seen him move that fast.

I felt like a little kid—pretending to be asleep when I wasn't. But I felt secure, and safe, and protected in the early-morning darkness, watching Dan go about his business. Somebody burned Avery's house down in another world. Not this world. Here, lying still and silent in the dark at Dan Sikora's, I was safe.

I heard the soft clink of a spoon against a cup as he stirred his instant coffee, and the sucking sound of the rubber seal on the refrigerator door as he opened it to get a carton of milk. He stepped into my line of vision again, and I lusted, unabashedly, for his body. For someone whose exercise regime seemed limited to sorting through boxes of old pictures and lifting the occasional radiator, he was in remarkably good shape. Not that I'm immensely picky—a look at Hugh would show you that. But there's something about drawstring pajama bottoms and nothing else on a guy that always does a number on my groin.

Dan's drawstring was riding low—just over his hipbones— and the knot swung, heavy and loose, below his navel. By the light from the open refrigerator I could see his torso at work while he poked around the kitchen—his back smooth and broad, his chest a thicket of rough brown hair. I remembered the smell of him and the feel of his chest beneath my cheek as we lay on Avery's sofa—when? Just five days ago?

I closed my eyes while he crossed the room toward his bureau, half willing him to stop by my sofa on his way. He pulled on a T-shirt and then a sweater.

"Dan?" I whispered. But he didn't seem to hear.

He was writing a note—to me, I suppose—on a piece of paper on top of the bureau.

My heart sank as I remembered my diaphragm, destroyed, I assumed, like my other belongings, in the fire at Avery's. Probably fused to the inside of my toiletries bag.

"Damn."

"Libby, is that you?"

He walked toward me.

"I'm awake," I said.

He lifted a box from the floor beneath the table.

"Libby," he said, "I've got to get to an auction in Sharon. I'll be back tonight. Maybe for dinner. Here's a key."

He was out the door before I could respond.

I lay on the sofa until five-thirty or so. Then I got up, switched on the lights, and made myself some coffee. The clothes that I'd hung over the radiator the evening before were damp at the edges and stiff in the middle, so I stayed in the hand-me-down sweats Sikora had given me.

I thought about the Vroman photographs that he'd shown me the night before, and decided to browse through them again over a slow breakfast.

I reached under the sofa where I'd seen Sikora put the portfolio, and pulled out, instead, a reddish-brown cardboard envelope—the kind that expands like an accordion—with a large black inkstain on the front of it. It looked familiar, but I didn't know why. I assumed it, too, had pictures in it, and I uncoiled the string from around the clasp to open it.

It was filled with family snapshots—a hundred of them, at least. I leafed through the first few, which weren't particularly interesting. Some out-of-focus snapshots from a wedding—someone getting married to a sailor; a few small photographs from the twenties of people playing on a beach; a little girl walking a dog on a leash, with the sun so strong in her face that it obliterated her features.

Some anonymous shapshots are worth saving—for the historical detail or maybe for a quirk in the composition that makes them interesting—but these weren't even unusual. I assumed they were Dan's family pictures and felt guilty for looking at them without his knowledge.

I was putting the handful of pictures back in the envelope when the thing slipped from my grasp and the entire contents fell to the floor. I bent down to scoop the pictures back inside, when one of them made me pause. It was a photograph of two boys standing next to an enormous snowman. The snowman had a carrot for a nose and a saucepan for a hat, and one of the boys was Dan Sikora. It was the same as, or similar to, the picture that was pinned to the bulletin board in Sikora's shop. But on this one someone had written in blue ballpoint pen around the margin: Teddy Struthers and Roger Struthers, Bridgeport, 3/2/55.

I brought the picture over to the light by the kitchen table and scrutinized the faces. There was no doubt about it—the boy to the left of the snowman was Sikora. He was one of those people whose adult features must have fully set in embryo. He looked as much like Dan Sikora when he was five years old and stuffed into a snowsuit as he did right now. I sifted through more of the pictures. Only one other had Sikora in it: He was in the back row of a group of ten or twelve high-school-age boys who posed under a banner that said BRIDGEPORT HIGH SCHOOL DIVISION I WESTERN LEAGUE HOCKEY CHAMPIONS 1966. The names of the hockey players were typeset underneath the picture, which must have been used for a high school yearbook. The boy third from the left in the back row, who looked like Dan Sikora to me, was identified in the caption as Ted Struthers.

Now I knew where I'd seen the ink-stained envelope before. Dan Sikora had taken it from the kitchen counter and carried it out of Avery's house the day I'd met him.

Why Ted Struthers? A conversation that I'd had with Sikora in his shop the first day I'd gone there rattled back to my head. The discussion about his business cards. The "T. Daniel Sikora." How he'd refused to say what the initial really stood for. "Theodore," he said. "But maybe Thomas."

Maybe his parents got divorced. Maybe his name was Theodore Daniel Struthers, and then his parents got divorced, or his father died, and his new father adopted him and he took the name Sikora. That would make sense.

But Bridgeport? He told me he'd lived in Arizona all his life. Bridgeport, Arizona? Snowmen in Arizona? Ice hockey in Arizona?

My mind kept darting back to that first afternoon in Sikora's store. He'd grown cold, even angry, when he realized I'd taken his picture. When I'd printed the roll, the pictures of Sikora had been wiped out. How?

Easy. He'd opened the back of the camera when I'd gone upstairs. He knew what he was doing. He didn't want anybody to recognize him from one of my photographs.

Something was wrong. Something was all wrong. My fingers trembled while I stuffed the pictures back into the en-

velope and wound the string around the clasp. I tried to jam
the envelope back under the sofa where I'd found it, but I
felt resistance. I groped under the sofa to push whatever it
was aside and felt something cold and metal and heavy, like
a gun.

Like a black steel revolver. My hand jerked back involun-
tarily, as though I'd unwittingly touched a tarantula or a
rat.

What was the line he'd given me that day back in Avery's
kitchen when I'd asked him why he was wearing hunting
boots? Something about not even being able to fish, because
he couldn't stand to kill the worms?

A gun?

I didn't know what to do with it. Literally. I'd never used
a gun, any kind, in my life. I take it back. Once Grandad took
me target shooting and the kick from the shotgun knocked
me over and I vowed I'd never shoot anything again.

Part of me wanted to shove it back under the couch and
pretend that nothing was up. So Dan Sikora has a gun. So
he has a lot of valuable things to protect.

Part of me wanted to stuff it into my sweatpants pocket,
run to Avery's truck, and drive like holy hell to New York
City. Who was Dan Sikora, anyway? Richard Speck? Ted
Bundy? Suppose he killed Avery. Suppose he was waiting
downstairs to kill me.

But I'd heard the van leave. I looked out the kitchen window to the parking area.

Of course it was gone. Nobody was hanging out by the
doorway.

I wished I had Lucas with me. Maybe he only had three
legs, but he had a full set of teeth.

I pushed the gun back underneath the sofa. Way back. Then
I made myself sit down and think.

Kevin Kogut was still missing. I couldn't run out on him.
I'd help Ted and Marianne find him, and then I'd run. Maybe
not to New York—not yet. Maybe I'd take Claire's mom up
on that offer of a Maine vacation.

I tried Ted and Marianne's number again. I figured if they didn't answer this time, I'd drive all over Darby until I found them.

It was busy. I hung up. A split second later the phone rang, setting off an explosion of adrenaline somewhere around my stomach. I lifted the receiver and said hello.

"Libby," the voice said. "This is Ted Dallas."

Thank God.

"Libby," he said, "we don't have any time to lose. I know where Kevin is. He called and asked me to bring you with me. I had a hell of a time finding you."

The words came out in whispery spurts, with long pauses between the sentences, when he sucked in his breath. Like somebody blowing up a rubber raft.

"I'll pick you up in fifteen minutes," he said, and then he hung up.

My eyes filled with tears of relief. So Kevin had been smart enough to call Ted after all. He must have called me, as he said he would, and gotten a busy signal, or a dead line, or whatever, at Avery's house. But he finally had the sense to call Ted.

But why did Kevin still think he needed me? Was he afraid of Ted? Did he want me there as a buffer because he was afraid that Ted would be angry with him?

I didn't know, and I didn't care. We were going to get Kevin; that was all that mattered.

I pulled on my jacket, hung my camera around my neck, and scanned the apartment for any more of my belongings.

My eyes landed on the sofa. I pulled out the red envelope and sorted through the pictures until I found the hockey team picture and the one of Sikora—or was it Struthers?—his brother, and the snowman. I laid them against the white sheet on Sikora's bed, braced my shutter arm on the top of the dresser, and took a picture. Not the best studio shot, but then, I'm not a studio photographer. Then I pulled out the gun, laid it next to the snapshots, and took a picture of the whole arrangement. It looked like the scene of the crime. Like a Weegee photograph.

What the hell was Sikora's story?

Ted Dallas would be here any minute.

I put the pictures back in the envelope, and slid the envelope and the gun back under the sofa. I locked the door behind me, went outside, sat on the concrete stoop in front of the shop, and waited for Dallas.

The street was absolutely still. No cars, no delivery trucks, no storekeepers arriving early to set up shop, no nothing.

It was cold, and the chill from the concrete spread through my sweatpants to my backside. I pulled Becky Bullock's jacket tighter around me and jammed my hands deep into the pockets.

The sky was still dark, but in the half-light from the streetlamp I could see my breath in clouds in front of my face. I puffed, pretending I was smoking an imaginary cigarette, wishing like mad that I had a real one.

Patsy Cline's voice swam around in my head:

> *Crazy*
> *For thinking that my love could hold you.*
> *I'm crazy for tryin'*
> *Crazy for cryin',*
> *And I'm crazy for lovin' you.*

A white cat slipped out from behind a cardboard box in a pile of trash across the street, pounced on something in the gutter, and vanished back into the trash.

Dallas pulled up in the dark-brown van with the sunset painted across the back that I'd seen parked in his driveway. I opened the passenger door and climbed in.

"Where did he call from, Ted?" I asked. "Where did Kevin say he was?"

"He wouldn't tell me where he was," he said. "But he told me where he'd be. I hope he got the directions right. That he knows where he is. That he doesn't move. That nobody moves him."

He fumbled with the gearshift, shot us into reverse by mistake, then rammed us back into drive.

"Did he sound like he was by himself?"

Ted rubbed a tear from his cheek with the back of his hand. "I sure hope so," he said. "If anybody did anything to him, so help me God, I'll kill them. I'll—"

He looked down at the dashboard. "Shit," he said. "No gas."

He looked terrible—like someone who hadn't slept, or bathed, or done a normal human activity in a week. His hair was uncombed, and when he pulled his hand away from the stubble on his cheek I noticed that he'd chewed his fingernails beyond the quick and that the cuticles were torn and scabby. His running shoes were caked with dirt, and the collar was folded in on his hunting jacket.

"What about Marianne?" I said. "Didn't she want to come?"

"Marianne," he said. "Marianne can't take it anymore. This is killing her. She's doped up. She's boozed up. She slept in the basement last night. I didn't even tell her he called. I'm not telling her anything until I've got him right here. Right here with me in the truck."

We pulled into a self-serve Mobil station. Ted sat, with his face in his hands, while I pumped the gas and paid for it. I climbed back in.

"I love the kid," he said. "He's not mine, but I love him. Even if I never tell him. Even if I'm kind of hard on him sometimes."

He let out a deep, shuddering breath, and then he pulled out onto Armstrong Road—a little too widely—so that we swung for a moment onto the shoulder of the road.

"Sorry," he said. "I'm not thinking straight."

"Of course you aren't," I said. "Do you want me to drive?"

"No," he said. "I can do it. I need something to concentrate on."

We fell into silence for three, maybe four miles. There were lights on in a few farmhouses, and a couple of stars in the sky. I tried to get the heater to work.

"Where did he call from?"

Ted was dreaming, lost in some cloud of guilt and worry.

"What?"

"I said, where did he call from? Did it sound like a pay phone or something?"

"I'm not sure," he said. "It could have been a pay phone. Some pay phone somewhere."

I couldn't bring myself to tell him that I'd talked to Kevin two nights before. That I'd talked to Kevin and I hadn't called Ted right away.

"So where are we meeting him?"

"South of here," he said. "About forty miles south of here. Down near the YMCA summer camp he went to last year."

He was holding the steering wheel like a drowning man gripping a life preserver.

"Maybe he's been there the whole time," he said. "Maybe he thought if he stayed away long enough, his real dad would come get him."

I touched my hand to his arm, and he shook it off.

"Nobody should have to go through what Marianne and I have been through this week," he whispered, almost as though he were talking to himself. "Nobody. Never. I want to whip the hell out of him."

I had never seen anyone in such a ditch of pain. I thought for a moment about all the parents of all those missing children whose faces you see on grocery store bulletin boards, and television news spots, and those milk cartons that Marianne's mother had talked about. It must be unmitigated hell for them. Ted was right; nobody deserved that kind of misery.

We lapsed into silence again. Ted turned off Armstrong Road and drove along a series of narrower country roads; past a chicken farm, past a reservoir, past a "Pure Comb Honey" stand.

Ted turned the radio to a Muzak station playing "Three

Coins in the Fountain." The dial slipped out of focus and he turned it back. It slipped out again and he turned the radio off.

I tried talking to break the tension.

"What do you know about Dan Sikora?" I said. "He wasn't at Avery's funeral. He didn't seem to be part of Avery's old gang of friends."

Dallas paused for a while, and then he took a pack of cigarettes out from behind the sun visor.

He lit one with trembling fingers and took a long, deep drag.

"I have to hide these," he said. "I can't let the kids see me smoking. I try, but I just can't quit."

I sympathized. "I know how it is. I haven't smoked in years, but sometimes I just want to hold one in my hands and smell it."

He wedged the pack behind the visor and took a couple more puffs.

"Sikora," he said. "He's okay, I guess. Avery thought so, anyway. Kind of keeps to himself, though. Kind of a loner."

He glanced over at me and then back to the road.

"You seem to like him okay."

A loner, I thought.

"Yeah," I said. "I like him okay."

Something about the landscape looked familiar. After a while a small yellow-brick building curved into view and I knew exactly where we were: at the Yannis gas station, five miles from Avery's fishing site. Ted must have taken me along a back route.

"Hey," I said. "I've been here before. This is right by where Avery used to fish."

"Right," said Ted. "I came with him a couple of times."

"So where's the camp? Did Kevin say he wanted to meet us at the camp?"

As we drove by the station, I saw the owner, the woman

who had given me the directions to Jarvis Beck, step out the front door and begin to wipe down one of the gas pumps with a rag. I waved to her and then felt foolish. Of course she wouldn't remember me. She didn't even seem to notice.

Dallas grew visibly tenser as we drove past the station.

"I didn't say he was meeting us at the camp," he snapped. "I said we were driving to a place near the camp."

"Sorry," I said. "I guess I didn't hear you right."

He ran his hand through his hair.

"I'm sorry too," he said. "I just hope to God he's where he said he'd be."

We continued on the route that I had taken to Jarvis Beck, past the dump and past the blue-metal garage building, the morning sun rising behind us as we drove. We drove on a half mile or so beyond the turn that led to the fishing site, and started down a steep, narrow road that paralleled the stream for a while, then took us quickly into a deeply wooded area. The surface was packed down harder than the roads I'd taken to Jarvis Beck. Packed down harder and impressed with wide, deep tire tracks. "What is this place, Ted? What goes on around here?"

"Lumbering," he said. "Black walnut trees. They're worth a fortune. The guy who owns this place must be rolling in it."

We drove on for another quarter of a mile, and then the road ended. Just like that. A road to nowhere.

Ted turned off the engine and sat for a moment, with his eyes closed. I wondered if he was praying.

Then he opened them again.

"Where is he, Ted?" I said. "Where did he say he'd be?"

"There's an entrance to an old mine tunnel over there where those stumps are," he said. "Kevin and I ran across it on one of our hikes at the YMCA camp. He said he'd be sitting just inside."

He was gesturing toward a group of tree stumps at the base of a small hill.

I replayed the drive we had just taken, past the road that went to Avery's fishing place, parallel to the stream for a while. Chances were, this was the old mine that Avery had been researching—the mine I'd seen the maps of.

"Avery knew about this mine," I said. "I think he used to come here."

Ted was staring straight ahead at the place he'd said was the mine entrance. He looked confused and anxious.

"Maybe," he said. "Maybe Kevin brought him here when they were fishing."

He reached beneath the seat and took out a flashlight—one of those shiny metal ones with a six-inch lens.

I followed him out of the van and over to the area by the foot of a small hill near the stumps he had motioned toward—an area overgrown by vines and bushes.

"Kevin! Kevin!" he yelled. "It's us! It's Avery's sister and me. We're going to bring you home!"

No answer.

I tried myself.

"Kevin, it's me, Libby! We were worried about you. Nobody's going to punish you. Where are you?"

Still no answer. Something made a noise in the underbrush by the car, and we both spun around at the sound.

"It's nothing," said Ted. "Maybe a pheasant." His voice was shaking.

He bent over and walked along the base of the hill, occasionally tugging at a vine or a branch. Finally, he reached down and pulled at a branch with both hands. A tangle of branches and brush the size of a car hood lifted away in one piece, revealing a hole in the side of the hill about ten feet across and five feet high, covered with a loose network of planks and boards. Dallas pulled away the boards and piled them on the ground.

"Ted," I said, "how could he be in there? It's too dark. How could he have pulled those boards into place from the inside?"

Dallas had already entered the tunnel.

"I don't know," he said. "But it's where he said he'd be. If you don't want to come, you don't have to."

I climbed in behind him, felt something give way beneath my feet, then felt firm ground again. Dallas shone his flashlight in my face.

"Watch it," he said. "This is an incline. Stand still for a minute and your eyes will adjust."

Fat chance, I thought. The only light in the place was the dim sunlight coming through the entrance. Once we started moving, we'd have no light at all.

Ted took me by the hand and guided me in. The ceiling was so low we had to hunch over to avoid hitting our heads. The walls felt clammy, and the floor was rough and rubbly with rocks I couldn't see.

Ted started calling Kevin's name, and his voice echoed back three times, low and mournful. The echoes cleared. We listened for a response, but none came.

We walked deeper into the mine, Ted holding the flashlight, and me close behind, trying to be calm. In the glow from Ted's flashlight, I could see that the ceiling was supported by old timber posts. I wondered how old, and how rotten. I reached my hand up and dragged my fingers along the surface. Bits of rock broke away.

We took a turn to the right, leaving the pale glimmer of light from the mine entrance behind us, advanced twenty feet or so, and took another right. We seemed to be in a small room. We crouched through a small passageway at the back of the room into another room, walked eight or ten feet, and then moved into another hallway—or had we returned to the original hallway where it had taken a turn away from the light at the entrance?

The air seemed warmer inside than it had outside, but maybe it was just me. Beads of sweat erupted on my forehead and dripped down through the rough patches that used to be my eyebrows. I took a disintegrating Kleenex from my pocket and rubbed it across my face. The sweat sprang back again.

I unzipped my jacket, and tried to quell a mounting wave of panic by reminding myself that we were going to find Kevin.

We're going to find Kevin. We're going to find Kevin, and he's going to be all right.

I tripped on a pile of rocks and fell to my knees. Ted turned, waited for me to recover, and continued walking.

"Kevin!" Ted called. "Kevin—it's me and Libby Kincaid. We're not mad, Kevin. We're here to take you home!"

The words banged back in a ghastly, muffled echo. We heard nothing from Kevin.

"He's not here, Ted," I whispered. "We must be in the wrong place. We're going to get lost if we go any further."

I could feel the blood pounding inside my ears.

Ted stood absolutely still, waiting for Kevin to speak. I ticked off the seconds in my head. Thirty, forty-five, a minute and a half. Kevin didn't respond.

"I can't stand it," he said. "What if he's dead in here? What if somebody killed him and threw him in here?"

There was a small explosion of sound somewhere near the ceiling, like a rock breaking loose. Or maybe a bat exercising its wings. I shivered.

"Ted," I said, "Avery knew something about this place. Something bad. Something that got him into trouble, I think. I found some research he was doing on water from the stream he fished in. He found some sort of contaminants there."

Ted started to walk, then turned toward me.

"Stand still, Libby," he said.

Then he left me, taking the flashlight with him. I was immersed in utter darkness.

For a moment I wondered if I had died.

He reappeared, only ten feet away, and shone the flashlight in my face.

"Sorry, Libby," he said. "I brought you here to find out how much you knew, and now I know."

He reached for his belt, or his pocket. He fumbled for an instant, and I hurled myself at him like a human cannonball. We both hit the ground at once.

My right arm cracked against something hard, and an excruciating, red-hot bolt of pain shot up my shoulder, while the entire mine went black. Dallas gasped for breath like a man who had just had the wind kicked out of him, which he had. I must have knocked the flashlight from his hand, and it must have busted when it hit the ground.

I leapt to my feet and ran as hard and as fast as I could into the darkness, holding my left hand out in front of me, until I hit a wall.

Rockets of light, blue and red and yellow, shot off in my head. I leaned against the wall and willed myself not to black out.

I tried to orient myself, but it was impossible. I wasn't sure what side of the room I'd been on when Dallas left me, and I had no idea where I'd run in the darkness. I'd read somewhere about how skiers feel when they've been buried in an avalanche—how they have no sense of which direction is up and which is down. It was like that: an avalanche of darkness.

But I had the wall. I inched along, hugging it, trying not to break an ankle on the loose rocks that filled the floor. The excruciating pain in my right arm subsided into a constant, exquisite throbbing that radiated from a point somewhere between my elbow and my shoulder.

I tried to remember what the diagram of the mine interior on Avery's map looked like, but it didn't help. All I could recall was something that looked like a spine: a central hallway with what looked like smaller rooms carved out along the sides. From the trip I'd taken with Dallas so far, it didn't seem like an accurate picture of the place I was in now. I felt my way along the wall, hoping that it would take me in a loop back to the entrance.

I had no way of knowing if Dallas was on my heels or in another section of the mine altogether. I wondered if the flashlight hadn't broken after all. Maybe the impact had just turned the switch or loosened the bulb. Maybe Dallas had it in his hands right now and was just waiting for me to wander near him.

I tried not to make a sound. I tried not to breathe.

I took a step forward, cracked my forehead on a timber beam, and let out an involuntary yelp and a stifled curse that richocheted off the walls like marbles in a pinball machine. I stood still and listened for Dallas, praying that the echoes had led him astray.

The beam was over the entrance to a small space with a ceiling about four feet high. I crawled inside and sat, cross-legged, on the floor, my back to the wall. I felt enclosed and, for the moment, safe.

The only sound I could hear was my own breathing, raspy and arrhythmic from my cold.

This is what it's like to be a blind person, I thought. I held my left hand out in front of my face and saw nothing. I leaned my head out into the room I had just been in and stared at the darkness. I thought that I could distinguish two shades of deep black, but that was all.

I sat still for ten minutes, maybe fifteen, listening.

Ted Dallas was trying to kill me. He must have set the fire at Avery's. He's trying to kill me because I know something I shouldn't. Just like Avery.

Just like Avery.

I waited for Ted.

I waited, and I listened.

My legs began to go numb beneath me. I heard Kevin's voice in my head. "I think somebody's trying to kill me," he'd said. "I'll call you at six o'clock tomorrow morning." What kind of man would try to kill a fourteen-year-old boy? What could the mine have to do with the contaminants Avery found in Jarvis Beck?

I reached beneath me to unfold my deadened legs. My

sweatpants were soaking wet. I felt along the floor around
me with my hand. There was a puddle of water to my right,
and the wall above it was wet and soft.

Water or something worse.

I pulled back my hand and wiped it on my shirt.

Avery didn't know any more than I did. He knew that some
sort of chemical was leaching into Jarvis Beck—something
bad enough and in big enough quantities to affect the insect
life on the water. He knew enough about this old mine to
locate the map. And somebody else knew that Avery was researching the mine. Sikora knew, of course. Avery had gone
to him to find out where to do the research. Why was Ted
trying to kill me? Because Sikora had tried and failed?

Avery knew, or somebody thought he knew, how the chemicals got in the water. And the knowledge Avery had was
enough to drive someone to murder. Once, anyway. Now
twice.

I thought about Kevin and shuddered.

Maybe three times.

The mine seemed to go on forever. From what I could remember of the diagram that came with the map, it had two
shafts to the surface—maybe more.

Avery had traced the chemicals to the mine. Somebody
was dumping them down the shafts. I thought of the tire
treads on the road that we'd taken on the way in. They were
huge—like the tracks of a flatbed truck. A flatbed truck that
someone used for transporting tanks of hazardous waste that
they dumped down the mine shaft in the middle of the night?
I thought about Sikora and his predawn travels, and the
nights I'd tried to call him but got no answer. If Sikora was
dumping hazardous waste down the mine, why was Ted Dallas trying to kill me?

Easy. They were in cahoots. Making easy money hauling
away some manufacturing plant's toxic leftovers.

I heard a brief rattling sound, like keys in a pocket, and I

looked toward the sound. At first I saw nothing, and then I
saw a faint, barely detectable shift of light, as though someone had lifted one gray plastic transparency from another.

I heard a shuffling sound.

It had to be Dallas—Dallas with a light. It wasn't strong
enough to be a flashlight, though. Something smaller. Like
his lighter. The Bic lighter that he'd lit his cigarette with in
the van.

For the third time that morning I wished to hell I still
smoked. Then I'd have a Bic lighter in my pocket too.

Dallas slid into view, and I barely suppressed a gasp.

I was right. He was holding the lighter, and he had one
hand cupped around the puny flame as if he were afraid a
breeze would knock it out.

The flame gave off far more light than you would expect a
lighter could. I wondered how far Dallas could see. Ten feet?
Thirty feet?

I buried my face in my lap, afraid that the white of my
skin would reflect too brightly. My breath sounded fast and
too loud; like a fireplace bellows, I thought. I took a breath
and held it, then slowly let it out, then another, counting all
the while. I could hear Dallas breathing and the sound of
rocks crunching under his weight.

Twenty breaths later, I looked up again. Ted had passed
by. I could see the light and the shadow of his back moving
down what seemed to be the central chamber.

"Libby!" he yelled. "Libby! You'll never get out of here
alive! I can board up the entrance, and you'll be dead in
three days!"

The words banged off the walls, the ceiling, my head.

"Libby," he hollered. "Nobody will hear you! Nobody will
help you!"

I smeared some dirt on my face, hoping I'd blend in with
the walls the next time Dallas swung his lighter my way.
Then I crawled out of my hiding place and shook my sleeping leg awake.

I pressed my back against the wall and edged slowly along

the corridor in the direction Dallas had come from. I moved five feet, then another five, planting each foot slowly and firmly on the ground before I moved again.

Not a sound from Dallas. Not a glimmer of light.

I took a step and fell into a depression filled with water and rocks, splashing as I went down and dislodging more rubble, which fell into the water.

Dallas materialized, lighter in hand, at the far end of the corridor—maybe eighty, maybe a hundred feet from where I'd fallen.

My heart froze.

The lighter illuminated the lower part of his face and nothing more. He was smiling.

I didn't know if he could see me, but I knew he'd heard the splash. He walked toward me, ten, maybe twenty feet. Then he raised his gun and aimed it in my direction.

I flattened myself against the ground and the gun went off with a shrieking, cracking sound like I'd never heard before. I lay rigid, my face pressed into the dirt, holding my injured arm against my body with my left arm, biting my lip, trying not to scream with pain.

A second shot split the air above my head while the first reverberated. White lights went off in my eyes, like someone taking flash pictures, and I felt as though I were falling through space. I gasped for breath and realized that for the past few moments I'd forgotten to breathe.

I waited for the next shot. Instead, I heard a low, roaring sound, like a train, or like the first rumbles of thunder at the start of a storm. The sound grew louder, and louder, and then a load of rocks and rubble blasted out of the ceiling. A rock cracked off the back of my head. Then a second volley poured out and, gagging on the dust, I tried to stand up, thinking absurdly for a moment that if I could do that I could run. Every time I got to my knees, something knocked me down again.

I grabbed at the walls with my good hand, trying to find

something to hold on to. Things were still falling from the ceiling: rocks, dirt, I didn't know what. I lost my balance and fell on my back, instinctively covering my eyes. Dust filled my nostrils, then my throat, and I choked and coughed, while the rumbling sound reached its peak.

Then suddenly everything was very still.

I pulled myself to my feet.

I was terrified to move and terrified not to move.

I took three steps forward, touched a wall, and sidled along it briefly. The right side of my face ached, and the pain in my arm had spread up my neck. My mouth was parched with fear and gritty with dirt. I wondered if Dallas was right. Could I last in here for three days without water? Better yet, could I drink whatever lay in puddles on the floor?

I imagined the *Daily News* headline: "Mine Collapses: Photo Gal Mushed."

And then I heard a moan. A long, awful sound. The moan again, and then two long, pained words:

"Help me."

I squinted into the direction of the sound and saw nothing but darkness.

"Here," he said. "Over here." And then the moan.

I dropped to the floor, my heart thumping wildly. What if he still had the gun? What if he was pretending to be hurt, and he still had the gun?

The moan turned into labored breathing, then a grunting sound, and then a soft clicking sound.

A small sphere of light erupted near the floor twenty feet from where I lay. Dallas still had his lighter.

"Help me," he said. "I'm dying."

"Where's the gun, Ted," I said. "Where's the gun?"

I got to my hands and knees.

"Ted," I said, "I'm not doing anything until I know where the gun is."

He raised the hand with the lighter in it a few inches into the air, then drew it back to his chest.

"Look," he said, "I don't have the gun."

I crawled toward him.

He lay on his side, his face away from me. His right arm was beneath his head, bent weirdly backward at the elbow. He clutched the lighter in his left hand. As far as I could tell, the rest of his body lay trapped under a timber beam and a pile of rubble. I didn't see the gun.

He moaned again.

I stood up and walked around his head until I could see his face. His eyes were shut, and blood trickled out of both nostrils. His lips were paler than his face.

"Give me the lighter, Ted," I said. "I can't do anything if I don't have any light."

He raised his hand with the lighter in it.

"Throw it to me, Ted," I said.

He jerked his hand. The lighter fell to the ground and went out. I dove for it. If Dallas was faking anything he would have gone for me then, but he didn't.

I lit the lighter. Then I backed up until I felt the wall, and leaned my back against it for support.

"What can you say, Ted?" I asked. "What can you say that will make me drag that beam off your legs?"

He didn't respond.

"Can you tell me that you killed Avery?"

He opened his mouth and closed it again. Opened it and closed it. Like a fish out of water, I thought.

Then a sound came out of the mouth.

"I didn't want to," he whispered. "I needed the money. I owed Sam Moldovan twenty thousand dollars."

Moldovan, or Mondavan, or something like that.

"He's a shark," he said. "Marianne got some money from her divorce. I told her I was investing it for her, but what I did was I gambled with it. I always had good luck before. I always had good luck. I couldn't face her. I couldn't tell her I lost it. So I borrowed from Moldovan to pay it off. He was charging me twenty percent, and then he made it thirty percent. He said he'd kill Marianne. He said he'd kill Marianne and Kevin both. Maybe he did kill Kevin. I don't know."

"You needed the money?" I said. "You needed money, so you were dumping some company's toxic waste?"

"It was supposed to be easy," he said. "I didn't want to kill him. But Kevin told me about tests that Avery did on the water. Avery was figuring it out. I had to stop it before he sent the results to anybody. I had to. I would have gone to jail."

I started feeling faint. I knelt down and put my head between my legs. Ted went on talking.

"I told him I wanted to see his gun. I told him I wanted to buy one. I shot him, and then the dog came, and I had to shoot him too. I wanted to shoot myself, but there weren't any more bullets."

"And then you wrote that phony note on the computer," I said.

He responded, but I didn't understand what he said. He moaned, and then he stopped talking. A rivulet of tiny, bloody bubbles oozed out of the corner of his mouth. He opened his mouth again, closed it, and opened it again. No, it wasn't like a fish, I thought. It was like a snapping turtle. The way they kept opening and closing their jaws after Grandad cut their heads off when he made turtle soup.

I put the lighter in my pocket and crouched by the beam that lay across Ted's legs. I pressed my left palm against the wood. Nothing budged. I hooked my arm around the end of the beam and tugged. I couldn't move it. I grabbed Ted by his good arm and pulled. It was useless. I might as well have tried to pull the driveway out from under a car.

I heard another rumble, and a bunch of rocks and dirt spilled from the ceiling onto the floor near my feet, as though someone had emptied a bucket.

I lit the lighter and held it by Ted's face. His pupils were dilated, his gaze fixed somewhere on the ceiling. I lifted his hand again. It was limp. I was pretty sure he was dead.

Another pile of rubble fell from the ceiling. I ran, as softly as I could, but as quickly as I could, terrified of triggering another collapse, to the other end of the chamber. I turned to the left, felt my way through a small, low-ceilinged room, turned left again, and found myself staring into the room at the entrance to the mine. I ran forward to the entrance, crawled out, and ran to Dallas's van, shielding my eyes against the afternoon sun.

I climbed into the van and sat, crying, in the driver's seat. My right arm had swollen so much that it was rigid inside my jacket sleeve, like a sausage in a casing. I looked in the rearview mirror. A dark-purple bruise the size of a pork chop spread from my right temple across my cheekbone. My face was filthy, and my bottom lip was swollen and raw. I had bitten through the skin trying to keep myself from screaming when my arm hurt in the mine.

No keys. I was in the van, but I didn't have any keys. I pounded the steering wheel with my good hand. I didn't have a clue how to hot-wire it. I took my camera from the floor of the passenger seat, hung it around my neck, and started up the road to the main highway. It was hotter than it should have been, given how cold the early morning had been. I cut through the woods to the stream, sat on the bank, and splashed some water in my face. I made a cup from my hand and drank, deciding that my chances of blacking out from dehydration were greater than my chances of contracting cancer from whatever it was that was leaching from the mine into the river.

I continued my trek to the highway, giddy with hunger and pain. When I reached the roadside, I stood still for a while, hoping that the next car would give me a ride. An elderly woman in a green Chevy passed me, then stopped. The bumper sticker to the left of her license plate said HIS EYE IS ON THE SPARROW. As I ran to the car, she got a better look at me in her rearview mirror, gunned her motor, and took off.

I walked slowly by the side of the road, breathing in the sunshine and open space like a sprung woman. The sky was crisp baby blue. The roadside weeds smelled fresh, wild, intoxicating. Even with the throbbing in my arm and the headache collecting behind my right eye, I felt euphoric.

Fifteen minutes later, a brown Ford pickup with a loose muffler slowed down, and a skinny kid wearing sunglasses leaned out the passenger window.

"You been hit by a car?" he said. Then, taking off his sunglasses for a better view, "Hey, don't I know you?"

It was the boy from Yannis's Beer, Gas, and Groceries. The boy with the scar.

He drove me to the gas station and got his mother. I sat on a stool by the cash register while she looked me over.

"Land sakes," she said. "Land sakes. Who did this to you?"

She poured me a juice glass of Wild Turkey, took a pair of scissors, and sliced the jacket off my arm.

I tried to tell her about Avery, and Ted, and the cave-in at the mine.

"Don't tell me any more!" she said. "Don't tell me! You went into that thing?" she said. "What are you, some kind of moron? Some kind of nut?"

She wrapped some ice in a rag and told me to hold it against my face. Then she called the police. I could hear her arguing with them. They wanted her to keep me there; she wanted to take me to a hospital.

"How in the hell do I know where the mine is!" she yelled into the receiver. "I'll put Tyrell on the phone. He knows more about geography than I do!"

She grabbed a Milky Way out of the freezer and stuffed it into my hand.

"Here, take this. You can eat it or you can hold it on your face."

She shunted me back to the truck and buckled my seat belt for me.

"I'd take you to the clinic, but you might end up worse off

than when you started, so we're going to the hospital instead."

I felt myself dozing off.

"Avery's sister, you said. Avery's sister. A dead man in the mine. Now I've heard everything."

17

They doped me up while they set my arm, then they rolled me into a room to rest. I was separated by a plastic shower curtain from my roommate, a woman who had both legs in casts and a tube running up her nose. My right arm was taped across my chest, my hand secured over my heart, as if I were about to pledge allegiance to the flag. Only my pinkie was free. I made a tiny salute with it.

I drifted in and out of sleep to the sounds of my neighbor's TV—"Wheel of Fortune," I think, and some news shows. An attendant brought me dinner on an orange plastic tray—soup, a little mound of raisins and shredded carrots pasted together with mayonnaise, and a slab of bright-green sherbet that melted before I could chew the spoon out of its plastic bag.

A nurse with a name tag that said "Florida" on it stabbed me in the hip with a syringe the size of a mailing tube.

"To help you sleep," she said.

"I thought I was going home."

"Not yet."

"Then when?"

"Not until we're sure your head is okay."

"Are the police here yet?"

A cop had taken a statement from me in the emergency

room, but the doctor said the rest of the interrogation would have to wait.

"You'll have plenty of time to talk with the police."

The tranquilizer spread from my hip to my toes to my ear-lobes, and for a while I had the sensation that I was floating above the bed, like a magician's levitating lady. I tried to focus my eyes on a calendar on the wall at the foot of the bed, but the numbers kept sliding apart. Then I didn't care about concentrating on anything anymore and fell asleep.

It was nighttime when I awakened. The room was dark except for a pale fan of light that spread across the floor from the half-open doorway. The only sound in the room was my roommate's snoring—deep and relaxed, like a dog's.

I felt a dull throb in my head and knifelike pain in my right shoulder. The bedsheet felt impossibly heavy against my chest—like the lead apron they'd laid on me when they x-rayed my head and arm. I needed more pain medication. I groped for the nurse's bell, then saw it lying, out of reach, across my feet. I pressed the button that elevated the head of the bed, and winced with pain as my torso rose forward.

The bell slid off the bed onto the floor.

"Shit!" I hissed.

Something moved in the shadows to the right behind my head. I turned my head and looked back as far as I could. Someone, a large someone, was sitting in the chair in the corner of the room.

"Libby? Are you all right?"

The voice was Dan Sikora's.

I could see the outline of his hiking boots and the lower part of his legs, but that was all.

I tried to talk, but nothing came out.

"Libby, I've been worried sick about you. I told them I was your brother."

If he knew that I'd seen the pictures and the gun in his apartment and linked him up with Dallas, he was playing it cool. Playing it cool—just like Ted—until he had a chance to kill me.

If he didn't know, I had a chance to play along with him.

"How did you know I was here?" I whispered. "How did you know I was hurt?"

"I drove by Ted Dallas's house on the way home, and there were cops all over the place. I thought maybe they'd found Kevin or something, so I stopped in, and they told me about you and Ted and the mine.

"I'm sorry," he continued. "I should have figured it out about Ted. I should have stayed with you. I'm sorry."

My roommate moaned.

Sikora lowered his voice.

"I can't believe it," he said. "He was a teacher. A coach."

It was the same thing people had been saying about Avery: I can't believe it. A teacher. Suicide. He was supposed to be a good example.

"Dan," I said, "do you know how to use a gun?"

Silence.

"I said, do you know how to use a gun?"

"Why, Libby?" he said. "What difference would it make? Why do you want to know?"

"I need to know, Dan. I need to know if you can use a gun."

He stood up and dragged the chair closer to my bedside, so I could see his face.

"Yeah, Libby," he said. "I can use a gun."

"Why do you keep one under the sofa?"

"I can't answer that, Libby," he said.

"If you can't answer that, then maybe you can answer this: Why did you open up the back of my camera and wreck the picture that I took of you in front of your shop?"

"Come on, Libby, what are you getting at?"

"And why is your name really Ted Struthers, and why did you say you were raised in Arizona if you're really from Connecticut, and one final thing . . ."

I was crying.

"Were you in on this thing with Ted? Did you kill Avery?

Did you kill Kevin too? Did you plant his library card in the field?"

Sikora leaned back in his chair and folded his arms over his chest. He stared up at the ceiling and shook his head slowly from side to side.

"Jesus, Libby," he said. "I can't believe this."

"I can't believe it, either," I said. "I was falling in love with you, and you're a killer."

"I knew it would have to happen," he said. "I knew somebody would find out."

Dear God, I thought. Help me. Make an orderly come into the room. Make the police show up and give me the third degree. Make lightning strike the building and kill us all at once.

"Libby," he said, "I'm going to have to trust you."

"What in the hell are you talking about?"

"I'm going to have to trust you more than I've trusted anyone in my life. More than Avery, even."

He stood up and looked down the hall. Then he stared at my roommate. She was snoring again. Deep, dead snores.

He sat down again at my side, and began to speak in a whisper.

"Libby, I didn't kill Avery. I don't have anything to do with Ted Dallas, or abandoned coal mines, or hazardous waste."

He poured some water from my bedside pitcher into a Dixie cup and drank it down.

"In 1968," he said, "I got involved in some left-wing politics. Nothing really radical," he said. "Not at first. Black armbands, antiwar protests, that was all. You remember, don't you?" he said.

There were footsteps in the hall—a passing nurse or an orderly. Sikora waited until the sound died away, then he got up and looked into the hall. He sat back down.

"Things got worse," he said. "Nixon ordered bombing runs into Cambodia. People were dying like insects. Kids, babies, men—we were hemorrhaging soldiers and murdering innocent people."

"I remember," I said.

"I was in school," he said. "In college. It seemed so small, so dumb. We thought we could shake things up. Shake things up and get the war to stop. I got friendly with a guy I'd known in high school. A rich kid. He was involved with some people who were . . . well, I guess we thought they were revolutionaries.

"His parents had a house at the beach. We went there for a weekend. To strategize, we said. Strategize and smoke dope, I guess. My friend and this woman spent the whole time in the basement. I was sitting on the porch, watching a meteor shower—sitting and watching a meteor shower—and the place blew up. Sky high. I got out. So did another guy. My friend and his girlfriend got killed."

"They were making bombs," I said. "They were making bombs, and there's no way you can ever prove that you weren't making them too, and besides, you probably knew that they were making bombs all along."

Sikora didn't say anything.

"You've been underground ever since," I said.

"I haven't seen my parents in twenty.years," he said.

"You kept that envelope of pictures and things at Avery's," I said. "I saw you take it out of his house. Did he know who you are?"

"No," he said. "I told him it was important that no one ever see it, and that was that."

"Is that why you opened up the back of my camera? Were you afraid that someone would recognize you from the photograph?"

"I'm sorry," he whispered. "I wrecked the film when you went upstairs to my apartment. I felt bad, but I had to do it. You get your pictures published all over the place. I couldn't risk it."

"In some ways," I said, "it's like you died."

"It is. It's like I died.

"Libby," he said, "I'm sorry Avery died. And I'm sorry you're hurt. I was driving you crazy. I knew Avery didn't kill himself. I knew you were right. But I knew that if I got involved in anything where the police were around—or where there'd be any publicity—"

"You'd blow your cover."

"I'd blow my cover."

"It's why you can't get into any legal battles with Bart Glass over the photographs."

"That's right."

I drew the sheet up over my bad shoulder.

"It's getting kind of cold in here," I said.

"Yeah," he said. "It's getting kind of cold."

He got up to go.

"Dan," I said, "can you do me a favor? Can you tell the nurse I need another shot?"

"Sure," he said.

"And Dan," I said, "can you do something else for me?"

"What?" he said. "Anything. What?"

"Can you go get Lucas at Pam Bates's and bring him to your place? It's driving me crazy, thinking of him cooped up in that pen."

"Sure, Libby," he said. "I'll go get him right now."

18

~~~

I'm at Claire's mother's house in Maine now, going for long walks on the beach and watching my hairline grow back in. I don't know how much Lucas is going to like Canal Street, but he loves it here and would spend all day retrieving rocks from the ocean, if I'd let him.

Dan Sikora drove Lucas and me to the airport for the flight east. It took some doing, but after I bought Lucas his own ticket and showed the proper people a note from Pam Bates, V.M.D., attesting to his recent life-threatening injury, they let him on the plane with me. I guess there's something compelling about a three-legged dog and a one-armed photographer.

Right before we got to the security gate, Dan stuffed an old tin box into my bag and told me not to open it until we were in the air. At sixteen thousand feet, I opened it up. Inside there were three Oreos, an egg salad sandwich, and a small square brown-paper package. I gave Lucas one of the Oreos and unwrapped the package, using my teeth and my good arm. A small hinged silver box molded in the shape of a woman's hand slipped out into mine.

It was a picture frame, designed to spread open and hold a picture on each side of the hinge. On the right, Sikora had inserted a black-and-white snapshot of Avery, wearing jeans

and holding a just-caught fish. On the left, he'd put a little
piece of folded-up white paper. I unfolded it and read:

> In his hand are the deep places of the earth: the strength of the
> hills is his also.

I think it's from the Bible, but I'm not sure.

I have the hand on my bedside table at Claire's mom's
house, along with my beach glass collection and alarm clock,
but I don't like to keep it open.

Sikora sent me a clipping from the *Marshall Post-Gazette*,
dated the day I left Darby. It said that Kevin Kogut came
home in the evening after Ted died, when he'd heard the
news on the radio. He'd plotted his own disappearance after
Ted threatened to kill him if he told anybody about the tests
Avery did on the water, and had been staying in a barn behind a friend's house in Salineville. The friend—someone he'd
met at camp—said that he'd planted Kevin's bike by the
school and the cards and picture from Kevin's wallet in the
field to throw Ted off the scent. The paper had a picture of
Kevin standing on the front steps of the Dallas house with
his arm around Marianne. "Kevin Kogut, 14, consoles mother,
Marianne Dallas, 35." According to the article, both Kevin
and Marianne were "shaken" by the week's events.

Claire flew up for the weekend with a bag of fresh mozza-
rella from Little Italy, a sack of mail, and the message that
Octavia had called me three times that morning. Something
about a cover story on Aretha Franklin and a shooting date
in three weeks. I've been out all morning, pitching rocks for
Lucas and practicing taking pictures with my left hand. It's
hard to get the film in, and harder to keep the camera steady,
but I'm getting the hang of it, and I'm not bad, not bad at
all.